DEADLY COINCIDENCE

Denise Richards

A KISMET™ Romance

METEOR PUBLISHING CORPORATION
Bensalem, Pennsylvania

KISMET™ is a trademark of Meteor Publishing Corporation

Copyright © 1991 Kim Shreffler
Cover Art Copyright © 1991 Alan Reingold

All rights reserved.

No part of this book may be reproduced, stored in a retrieval system, or transmitted in any form, by any means, including mechanical, electronic, photocopying, recording or otherwise, without prior written permission of the publisher, Meteor Publishing Corporation, 3369 Progress Drive, Bensalem, PA 19020.

First Printing May 1991.

ISBN: 1-878702-43-2

All the characters in this book are fictitious. Any resemblance to actual persons, living or dead, is purely coincidental.

Printed in the United States of America.

To the men in my life: Rick, Ricky and Trent

DENISE RICHARDS

Denise lives in the Texas Panhandle, where she has lived most of her life, with her husband Rick and their two sons, Ricky and Trent. Being an avid reader (at least one book a day, sometimes two), writing was a natural progression of her love of reading. In addition to writing, Denise finds time to travel, sew, bake, do crafts, and play the piano.

PROLOGUE

Timothy Bannion absently flipped the page of his newspaper and sipped his coffee. It was a clear day and he enjoyed playing tourist in London. The sidewalk café was crowded, just the way he liked it. No one paused to give the frail young man a second glance. There was no reason for anyone to see the evil lurking behind his clear blue eyes. No one to suspect he was responsible for the bombing outside the House of Commons yesterday. Too bad he had missed his target, but the three innocent dead should haunt the Prime Minister for a while. He twinged at the thought of the little girl that had been blown apart, but such was the way of war. Not that he really gave a damn about this war or any other. It was the killing he craved. The planning, the execution, the money. His employer had offered him triple his usual fee for a dead Prime Minister and that irritated him. He would have to try again in a few weeks.

Had to give Scotland Yard time to get lazy. He smiled as he thought of all the cops staking out Heathrow and every other airport and train station in the area. Any fool would know that it would be suicide to try to get out of London right now. And Timothy Bannion was no fool. The newspaper said that a radical Iranian group had claimed responsibility for the bombing and that was fine with him. He didn't need the glory.

He surveyed the other diners and his eyes came to rest on the American across the aisle. He listened while she ordered tea and crumpets. Probably thought she was acting like a native. Still, he rather liked her accent. It was soft and lazy; she must be from the southern United States. Her hair glinted in the sun and he casually checked her out. He found his gaze returning to her full breasts. He had tired of the thin, boney women he had been satisfying himself with lately. The redhead glanced up at him and smiled. Timothy grinned back and raised his cup in a silent salute. Maybe this would be his lucky day. He stared and she blushed and turned away.

Bannion picked up his half empty cup and started to make his way to her table. He would ask to sit with her, maybe show her a few of the sights. All she could say was no. With his eyes on the woman, Bannion didn't notice the large man barreling down on him. "What the bloody hell?"

"Pardon me! I hope I haven't injured you." The man was grossly fat and Timothy had to struggle under his weight. Trying to steady the man, Timothy felt the tip of the man's umbrella gouge painfully into his leg. "Oh, I've scratched you. You must let someone inspect it."

"Get lost," Bannion growled and strained to see around the man. Damn, the redhead was gone, she hadn't even waited for her order to arrive.

Timothy sat down at his table and ordered another cup of coffee. His leg stung a bit and he swiped at the cut with his napkin. He quickly drank the coffee, hoping it would give him a lift. He felt the last few hours catch up with him. Maybe it was time to make his way to an inn and get some sleep. He would have liked the pretty American to help him relax. Stupid fat idiot.

The London *Times* ran a small article on the death of Timothy Bannion, soldier of fortune. His death had been ruled a homicide. The autopsy had revealed a trace of coral snake venom in his bloodstream. Severe discoloration of the skin around a small scratch on his left leg upheld the theory. After all, one didn't run into coral snakes in the center of London. Bannion had been found dead in his hotel room by a maid. Scotland Yard had no suspects. A man like Bannion had a thousand enemies. In truth the officials weren't looking very hard. After all, someone had done the world a favor. Bannion had been responsible for dozens of terrorist attacks. His name was merely added to the file that had been steadily growing over the past three years. A file filled with dead terrorists and mercenaries. Each killed expertly, sometimes painfully, always deservedly.

ONE

Blue eyes burned into her green ones as he lowered his full lips and seared her mouth with a kiss. His long fingers twined in her coppery curls and she strained against him . . .

Laurie had no idea how long she had been sitting at her computer daydreaming. The stack of files on her desk was considerably lower than when she had started, so she must have accomplished something. Her eyes burned and there was a decided crick in the left side of her neck. Sliding back in her swivel chair she tried a few stretching exercises to relieve the tension. The suite of offices had been empty for sometime now and she was alone. When the ice storm had hit midafternoon, she had allowed the stores in the mall to close and send their employees home. Frankie, the maintenance supervisor, had left at five and she had assured him that she would be perfectly safe with the security guard for protection. Glancing at her watch she realized that had been three hours ago.

Laurie padded in stocking feet to the filing cabinet in the closet between her office and the mall manager's. James Conway had announced on Monday that he would be gone for a month to the Virgin Islands on a working vacation. The mall had recently been purchased by a development company out of Houston and they were treating the head honchos to this little treat. Since marketing and public relations fell second in line, Laurie was responsible for her job and Conway's. She had spent the last few nights catching up on the mountain of paperwork James had left on his desk. She did her best; unfortunately, her expertise was in dealing with people and ideas, not rent collection and broken toilets. With Thanksgiving only a week away her job of preparing the mall for the Christmas season took all of her time and she resented Conway leaving her with his unfinished business.

Picking up the phone, Laurie punched the button that automatically dialed her home phone. Her sister, Pitsie, had called earlier but she just felt the need to check on her. They had been receiving several disturbing phone calls at the house lately and, while Laurie wasn't overly concerned, she hated for Pitsie to be home alone. Snuggling the receiver with her shoulder, Laurie tried to straighten the mass of papers and files scattered on top. The menial task allowed her mind to drift back to that incredible looking man she had spotted this morning.

He had been sitting outside the Cookie Muncher talking with Henry when she had gone on her coffee break. She had almost tripped over her size sixes when he had pierced her with those neon blue eyes. She had realized immediately that he wasn't one of the regular mall walkers. Not one of the homeless that often wandered in out of the cold Panhandle weather on mornings such as these either. His flannel shirt was faded and his jeans soft and worn, but they were clean and pressed. His hair was a shining mass of chocolate brown waves and he didn't sport the usual early morning beard.

Against the darkness of his tanned skin and hair, his eyes were so pale they were almost translucent.

Laurie had spent a great deal of time during the day pondering her unusual reaction to the man. Normally she had to date a man twice before she noticed what color his eyes were. Her friends claimed they were happy if she even noticed the sex of a particular person. While that might be a slight exaggeration, Laurie freely admitted that she wasn't interested in romance of any kind. Didn't have the time or the inclination for the amount of work a relationship called for.

If any of her friends knew that she had spent half the day fantasizing about the way that flannel shirt had clung to his broad shoulders, or the way his subtle cologne haunted her, they would have either had her committed or thrown a party. Laurie couldn't explain the thrill that had stunned her every time he had glanced in her direction. There had just been something special in that intense gaze he had turned on her. Some connection that went beyond the normal male-female reconnaissance. They hadn't spoken, hadn't even acknowledged each other, but Laurie had never been more intensely aware of another person in her life.

In her flight from reality, Laurie failed to notice that the phone wasn't ringing. A few minutes of button pushing and cord jiggling confirmed that the line was dead. "I don't believe this."

This was the third time this week that there had been trouble with the phones. James had assured Laurie that he would see to the repairs personally. That was before he had been ordered to the Islands, of course. Once he had received his orders, he had made her ill with his banal conversations concerning his wardrobe.

Slipping into her long wool coat and matching green scarf and gloves, she felt ready to brave the bitter Panhandle cold. Double checking her office, she concluded that all was ready for business on Monday and stepped into the dimly lit hallway leading to the mall's center court area.

Being in the mall at night always reminded Laurie of going to school for open house. There was an odd excitement about being in the huge building alone. Especially when it was normally filled with people. A few of the stores were delicately lit so the guard could check for customers doing a little after hours' shopping. Her snow boots made virtually no sound on the tile floor as she quickly crossed to the large sliding doors leading to the north parking lot.

Her key fit neatly into the slot, but when she pushed on the automatic doors, nothing happened.

Laurie laid her purse down and tugged off her gloves. Hands on the door, she pushed hard. Still nothing. Standing in front of the door, hands on hips, she assessed the situation. Suddenly it became clear. Crystal clear. The north wind had deposited about an inch of ice over the city. Through the prismlike quality of the doors, Laurie viewed the deserted parking lot. Her compact car stood like a monument to her stupidity under one of the security lights.

Gathering her belongings, she trudged across the mall to the south side. The wind had been from the north, so the southern exposure should be fairly clear. The southern doors, however, were wrapped with a large chain and she didn't have a key. Scanning the other exits, she realized that the only one that might possibly be unchained or free of ice was the delivery door.

The corridor that ran behind the stores was brightly lit, but due to the short business day, was abnormally tidy. Laurie missed the stacks of boxes and packaging she normally shuffled through when using the hallway. The white cinder block walls held the cold and Laurie wrapped her scarf around her throat. Her boots made sticky noises on the concrete flooring, so the hard clip of a boot was easily distinguishable. She stopped and listened. The footsteps stopped. The fine hairs on the back of her neck prickled and she found herself holding her breath. Cautiously, she began walking and the footsteps resumed. Picking up her pace, she realized that someone was behind her. Not daring to glance around, she rounded the corner leading to the back hallway. Adrenalin pulsed through her and she forced herself to slow down. If someone was following her, they would catch her easily before she could unlock the heavy steel door at the other end of the corridor. She stood still listening to the nearing footsteps like a victim in a horror movie. She wrapped her purse strap around her hand and prepared to swing it at the next person to round the corner. What she wouldn't give for a concealed weapon about now.

Tensed and ready, Laurie noticed that the footsteps had taken on a stop and go rhythm. They were coming closer, but whoever it was didn't seem in any hurry. Maybe she had time to reach the door and avoid any confrontation.

A cold wind brushed along her leg and she glanced over her shoulder and noticed the exit door closing. Someone must have come into the hallway while she had been concentrating on the footsteps, which had almost reached her. Sweat trickled down her back and she wondered where in the heck the security guard . . .

"Oh for Pete's sake," she admonished. The security guard. That was who the footsteps belonged to, not some ax-wielding murderer in a ski mask. Turning back toward the hallway, she decided luck was with her after all.

A leather-clad hand covered her mouth before she could utter a sound. The fingers bit cruelly into her delicate skin as her assailant forced her head up and back until she was pulled flush against him. Even wrapped as they both were, Laurie could feel the power of the man holding her. She instinctively tensed for retaliation. "Don't be stupid."

The words, barely audible, didn't penetrate the anger flooding her. The knife suddenly pressed to the base of her neck did. Even if she tried to outmaneuver him, she might end up with a sliced windpipe, or at the very least a severed artery. Instead of wasting precious time and energy trying to struggle, she began to catalogue any information she was able to gather concerning her attacker.

Male, over six feet, at least two hundred pounds. He was holding the knife in his left hand and he smelled of fear and Aramis. "That's a good girl. I'm just delivering a message. Play it smart and there won't be any need to baptize my friend."

He traced the knife blade against the hollow of her throat and Laurie felt the lethal tip jump as it lingered on her carotid artery. "Wouldn't take much would it?"

Laurie gently shook her head. Where was that stupid security guard. Wasn't this what he was paid to prevent?

"We want the package back."

Laurie grunted.

"Shut up." The leather hand pressed harder against her mouth and nose, cutting off her air. "Make sure you return the package exactly like you found it. We'll call you when we're ready to pick it up."

Laurie tried to shake her head again. Tried to make him understand that she didn't have any idea what he was talking about. This was like a bad joke.

The man mistook her shake for a struggle and the knife slid under her skin. "Don't make the mistake of thinking you are necessary. I have orders to kill you if you don't cooperate. I'm sure you understand all about orders."

DEADLY COINCIDENCE / 17

The pressure of his hand lessened and Laurie sucked in great gulps of air through the small slits of his fingers. In an instant the knife was gone. Laurie took a second to calculate the risks involved in hand to hand combat with an armed enemy. A second was too long. The leather curled into a fist and smashed with deadly accuracy into Laurie's jaw. Blinding lights exploded behind her eyes and pain flared through her brain. She watched the walls shift and melt before her. A low moan echoed from her as she slid to the floor. Then came the blessed darkness.

J.D. jiggled the lock of the kitchen shop's back door. Even though his job as a security guard was a terrific cover, it was boring as hell. He went through the motions of checking each door just in case Laurie happened to be watching. He had watched her enter the hallway a few minutes ago and decided to follow. Since he hadn't heard the outer door open, he figured she was still in the building.

The door to the store room was open and he decided to check it out. It was doubtful that she had come in here, but he needed to grab a quick look at the lay-out of the room anyway. Rather than turn on the overhead fluorescent lighting, he unhooked his flashlight from the utility belt that was part of his uniform. The strong beam of light penetrated the darkness and he quickly scanned the room. Nothing special. A few crates stood in one corner by a row of shelves filled with decorations and promotional material for the mall. There was another door on the other side of the room but it was chained from the inside. If Laurie had come in here, it wasn't with the intention of leaving. He flashed the light into the corners. No sign of anyone. Especially not a red-haired munchkin in a bright green coat.

A muffled noise caught his attention and he flipped

off his light. The room was as quiet as a tomb. Stepping back into the brightly lit hallway, he resumed his doorknob jiggling. Another noise. A smack really, sort of like someone popping gum. He inched closer to the cross section of the hallway. His muscles bunched, preparing for use. Releasing the snap on his holster, he slid the revolver out of its leather cradle. The weight felt odd in his palm and he reformed his grip. Amazing what five years of clean living could do to old habits. At one time his hand had felt naked without the cold steel clenched in his fingers. A moan drifted into the silence and he cautiously stepped around the corner.

His mind took in the scene and computed the best course of action in a matter of seconds. At least some of those old habits hadn't died. The exit door had just clicked shut and J.D. bounded over Laurie's prostrate body and sprinted after her attacker. On this ice he couldn't have gotten far. Tugging on the door the realization that it was locked slammed into his brain. His oath was raw and to the point. By the time he located the proper key among the mass hanging on his belt the assailant would be long gone.

Snapping his gun back in place, he hunkered down next to Laurie. Her jaw was already swollen and purple. He swore again and cast a look at the door. What kind of a jerk decked a woman? Get a hold of yourself, man, this isn't just any woman we're talkin' about here! J.D. unclenched his fist and forced himself to take a couple of deep breaths. Damn, he didn't care if the redhead did rank at the top of Interpol's wanted list, a man didn't hit a woman. Especially not one this soft and pretty. Drug her, yes. Shoot her if he had to. Even hog-tie her to a telephone pole. Anything but hit her.

Laurie moaned and turned her head to the side. J.D.'s gut quaked when he noticed the steady trickle of blood running down her neck. "The son of a—"

Laurie heard someone cussing and thought he really should watch his language around a lady. Maybe she was the one doing the cussing? The way her head hurt, she was entitled to a few off-colored phrases. No, the voice was deep and lazy. Laurie had practiced too long to overcome her Texas drawl. Even in extreme pain she wouldn't revert to that slow, melodic way of speaking. Maybe it was the man who had threatened her? Had he decided an uppercut wouldn't do the trick and wanted to call her a few ugly names? Did that make sense? Her head was spinning and she felt like a character in a foreign movie. Strange lighting and even stranger plot.

Gentle fingers probed along her neck and then a pressure. Suddenly she recalled the knife and the leather gloves. Her mind raced and the surge of adrenaline coursing through her gave her the advantage she needed. The man must think she was still unconscious. Peering through her thick lashes, she tried to get a fix on the man. All she could determine was he had shiny brown hair and was unbuttoning her coat. His large hands slid over the expanse of her stomach and thighs. Dear Lord, was he going to kill her and then rape her? He leaned down to press his head to her breast. Laurie raised her right hand and delivered a resounding whack to the side of his head. Thrown off guard the man struggled to regain his equilibrium. She deftly brought her knee into his chest and sent him sprawling.

TWO

J.D. blinked hard to clear his head. His lungs fought for the air that had been thrust from them and his hand went to his holster. Empty.

"That's right, buddy. Your little friend has found a new home." Laurie stood directly over him. The barrel of the gun pointed at his head. "Now suppose you do some talking."

"Lady, what are you doin'?" J.D. ignored the gun and pushed himself into a sitting position. "I just found you lying on the floor. When I saw all that blood on your neck, I thought you were dead. I was checkin' your pulse."

"Nice try." Laurie absently reached up to swipe at the sticky liquid staining a trail down her chest. She wanted to glance down at the blood covering her fingers, but knew she didn't dare take her eyes off this guy. "Move your hands so I can get a good look at your face."

J.D. had been rubbing his eyes, trying to get them to focus. He slowly lowered them and stared up at Laurie. He knew the second she recognized him.

"You're the man from this morning!" Terrific, she

thought, I spent the day fantasizing about a lunatic. "What were you doing, casing the joint?"

J.D. grinned up at her. "You sound like you've been watchin' too many E.G. Robinson movies."

"I do not think you are in any position to be making disparaging remarks." She waggled the gun for emphasis.

"Sure, sweetheart." He managed to get to his feet without making a fool of himself. "Look, Ms. Morrison, I'm the new security guard. I was checking the doors in the back hallway. I heard something, and when I came around the corner, there you were."

"Did you see anyone else?"

"No. The outside door was just closing when I found you. I figured whoever it was would've hightailed it outta here by the time I figured out which one of these keys unlocked the damn thing."

"Watch your language. I heard enough of that while I was regaining consciousness." Laurie didn't realize how prudish she sounded, especially to a man who suspected her of international terrorism.

"Well, excuse me, Miss Priss." He tipped an imaginary hat to her.

Laurie's eyes bore into his as she weighed the evidence. Her mind went over what she knew about her attacker. The man before her stood a few inches over six feet and probably tipped the scales at two hundred and fifteen. Since she wasn't sure how long she had been out, the man could have had plenty of time to get rid of his coat and gloves. Well, there was one other piece of information she could remember.

"I promise I'm tellin' the truth, lady. Do I look like I get my jollies punching women out?"

How the man got his "jollies" didn't bear contemplation right now. "What kind of cologne do you wear?"

The question threw J.D. off balance. "What?"

"Cologne! What kind do you wear?" Laurie felt her

blood soaking into the thin material of her blouse. She wished he would hurry up and convince her of his innocence. "I'm not blessed with an abundance of patience right now."

"I don't know what kind it is." J.D. shrugged. "Just something my sister gave me for my last birthday."

Laurie waved the gun at him. "Come here."

" 'Scuse me?"

"I said get over here." Laurie involuntarily stepped closer to him.

"Yes, ma'am." J.D. closed the gap between them with two long strides. He felt the muzzle of the gun jab into his ribs. "Careful, darlin'."

"Lean down here so I can smell you." His masculine scent was already wafting down to her. Strong and clean, nothing at all like the man who had hurt her. "I . . . uh. . . I need to . . ."

Her voice died a sudden death as J.D. bent down and offered his scent for her inspection. "You were sayin'?"

"Yes, I need to see if you smell like . . ." Her voice trailed away again as she breathed deeply of him. His hands had come to rest gently on her shoulders. She lowered the gun from his midsection. "I need to . . ."

"I need, too, sweetheart," J.D. rumbled in her ear as he tenderly caught her ear lobe between his teeth. "I need to do this."

She stiffened and turned to protest. Before she could scold him, he caught her mouth with his.

J.D. felt her tension evaporate, and he tightened his arms around her as she flowed to him for support. His body surged with the rush of power he experienced. He hadn't planned on kissing her just yet. He had carefully planned his strategy concerning the lovely Ms. Morrison. He had expected to become involved with her on some level. A kiss was almost inevitable. The possibility of even greater intimacy had crossed his mind and he was prepared. What he wasn't prepared for was the onslaught of foreign emotions flooding his brain. At this moment he wasn't sure where he stopped and she began. His fingers found the cool of her hair and his tongue the heat of her mouth.

Laurie's mouth opened of its own volition, her body craving the taste and feel of this man. Her mind struggled to stem the heat flaring through her.

Slowly his lips left hers and he placed a feathery kiss on the tip of her slightly upturned nose. Laurie successfully fought the urge to bury her face in his neck and nibble at the soft skin just beneath his five o'clock shadow. She ought to slap him silly, but realized that would be childish. The kiss had been a mutual collaboration. She could have stopped him at any time. After all she had the gun. The fact that she hadn't intrigued them both.

J.D. tensed, waiting for her to slap him or scream rape. Nothing. He was still holding her against him and she wasn't even struggling. That bothered him. Any normal woman would be having a fit about now. Any woman except one trained to handle this type of situation.

When Clifton had called him the first of the week with this assignment, he had tried to turn him down. He hadn't had an active case load in five years and he wasn't looking to start one now. Clifton had assured him the evidence against Laurie was strong. Merely a matter of a few days' surveillance and a couple of carefully conducted searches to put this little redheaded terrorist behind bars.

When her dossier had been delivered to him, he had skimmed it and cursed his superior. In the fifteen years he had been with the Technical Anti-Terrorism force (TAT), he had only screwed up once. Once was enough to ruin his career and his peace of mind. His entire world had been turned upside-down because of a woman.

A woman whose memory haunted his dreams and kept him from leading a normal life. He had fought desperately to escape the cesspool of the dark world that had been his playground. Now here he was fighting to keep his balance.

Laurie clenched the front of his shirt and managed to regain her composure. Her fingernail absently scraped against a dark stain on the front of his khaki shirt. "Oh."

"Oh? That's the best you can do?" J.D. smoothed the top of her hair under his chin. A strand of hair caught between his lips and he ran his tongue over it. He could taste her hairspray and he inhaled her scent. He could have held her all night. Man, he was losing his mind. He was standing in a cold hallway, holding a woman who had just been attacked and was bleeding all over the front of his shirt and all he could think about was how she felt in his arms. He better put a call in to Clifton in the morning and tell him to get some other jerk to finish this assignment. "We'd better go check on that cut and call the police."

Laurie tipped her head back to look at him. "I guess so. I don't know what good the police can do. I didn't see the man and I have no idea what he wanted."

J.D. refrained from explaining to Laurie the things a man would want to do with her. "Can you remember anything about him?"

"A few things." Laurie pressed against her temple to quell the ache in her head. "He was about six feet, around two hundred pounds. I can't really be sure about the weight because he was wearing a coat. He held a knife in his left hand and he wore Aramis cologne."

"That's pretty impressive." J.D. tried to stop the uneasiness nettling him. "Most people wouldn't have been able to give that much of a description."

Laurie shrugged and started back down the hallway.

"It just seemed important that I be able to identify him."

"I'm sure the police will appreciate it." J.D. took hold of her elbow. "Come on, let's go get you cleaned up."

Laurie was grateful for his support. "Thank you . . . Good grief, I don't even know your name."

"It's J.D. J.D. Westat."

"Well then, thank you, J.D. I don't know what I would have done if you hadn't come along." Laurie shuddered just thinking about what might have happened to her if the man hadn't heard J.D. coming.

"From what I saw back there, I'd say you were pretty damn good at taking care of yourself." J.D. slipped his key into the office door and held it open for her.

"You certainly do cuss a lot."

"Does it bother you?"

"A little. I spent five years trying to convince my little brother that profanity was a sign of ignorance." She grimaced at his expression. "I'm sure that's not why you do it."

"Think not, huh?" J.D. tried to maintain his stoic face.

"No, I think you've just been around some pretty rough people and that was a good way to fit in."

Laurie shocked J.D. with her perception. He had hung around the other security guards and patterned his speech and actions after them. He had always found the best way to maintain a personality undercover was to employ their habits. So for a week now he had been hanging out at night clubs with a couple of the guards, studying them. As for the cussing, well that really wasn't too out of character.

Laurie led him into her office and flipped on the light. "I've got a first aid kit around here somewhere."

"You want me to call the cops?" J.D. picked up the receiver without waiting for a reply. "The phone's dead."

"Still?" Laurie crossed the room to where J.D. was standing and took the phone from him. "This has been happening all week. My boss was supposed to make sure it was fixed before he went on vacation." Her tone of voice left no doubt as to her opinion of her boss. She slammed down the receiver and flopped into her chair.

J.D. busied himself with the first aid kit. Her eyes were suspiciously bright and there was nothing in the manual about how to handle a crying terrorist. The uneasiness he had been experiencing since this assignment had been thrust on him resurrected itself. He had survived for years on his instincts. Strange feelings and gut reactions weren't taught in the training courses, but they were what had enabled J.D. to reach the ripe old age of thirty-five. J.D. had learned to listen when his "little voice" had something to say. Right now it was saying he shouldn't be condemning Laurie without irrefutable evidence. At least he hoped it was his instinct and not his hormones.

Laurie wiped her tears off her cheek before J.D. saw them. "I'll call the police when I get home."

Her voice was dull and J.D. knew that her rush of adrenaline had dissipated, leaving her drained. "Let me take care of that neck, darlin'."

He knelt down in front of her and poured hydrogen peroxide onto a clean gauze pad. "This might sting a bit."

Laurie's eyes held his for a second and she nodded. "I'll be fine. Just do whatever you have to."

J.D. wondered if she was aware of the double meaning in her words. Doing what he had to do, meant proving that she was responsible for several deaths in Europe and the Middle East. He stared at the dried blood marring her flesh. "I'm gonna have to unbutton your shirt."

She nodded and tilted her chin up to give him better access. He fumbled with the tiny pearl button, almost ripping it off in his clumsy attempt. She reached up and gently pried his fingers off the button. "I'll do it."

J.D. had trouble swallowing around the lump that had suddenly formed in his throat as he watched her shiny pink fingernail slip the pearl through the slot, exposing the lush curve of her breast. Grinding his teeth together to stop his inane thoughts from spilling out, he quickly tucked the collar of her blouse under the lace-edge of her bra.

"I'll be through in a second," he said more to himself than to her. He found his gaze drawn to a tiny freckle nestled at the top of her cleavage. He could smell her perfume as it mixed with the metallic odor of blood. "Just let me get this bandage taped in place."

When Laurie didn't answer him, he glanced up. Her head had fallen to her left shoulder and a strand of her coppery hair was laying across her eyes. J.D. reached up and brushed it back. She looked so innocent, he couldn't help but wonder how a pretty little girl from west Texas ended up an international killer.

When he had first seen her at the mall this morning he figured there had to be a mistake. She had walked straight towards him and for a second he had thought his cover was already blown. She had tossed him a semi-smile and walked past him to the Cookie Muncher. He had been sitting in the same chair nursing the same cup of coffee all morning. Waiting for her. He watched her buy a cookie and cola from the guy behind the counter, laughing like she didn't have a care in the world. He figured she didn't realize TAT had a tail on her and his job would be simple. He had pretended to watch the elderly people taking their morning constitutional in the warm dry mall. One gray-haired gentleman had immediately struck up a conversation once he noticed the way J.D.'s eyes kept finding Laurie.

"She's a pretty little thing, isn't she?"

J.D. had agreed wholeheartedly and then sat back while Mr. Greenhaw had sung Laurie's praises. In the space of a few minutes he had learned that Laurie was considered a paragon of virtue. Henry proudly informed him that she didn't even "sleep around" like most of these youngsters today.

J.D. had only half-listened to the man as he watched every move Laurie made. Her hair glistened like a raindrop in the sunshine. It was shaped into one of those wavy hair cuts that was all the same length, a bob or page boy, something like that. The dossier had stated she was 5'1" and weighed 120 pounds. He admired the way nature had distributed each and every ounce. Her walk had just the tiniest bit of a jiggle that made it pure enjoyment. Even her plain tailored blouse and matching purple straight skirt looked like something he had seen on a burlesque dancer as a kid. When he had spotted her matching high-heeled shoes he had all but thrown himself at her feet. She had sat down next to Henry and when she glanced at him with those eyes, he had found himself lost in their green-gold depths. He had decided right then and there she was innocent. After what had happened tonight, he decided he had better listen to his instinct. Someone had wanted something from her. He would bet his last dollar that the attack wasn't some random crazy looking to prove his manhood. The cut on her neck had been done by an expert. Someone who knew just where and how deep a cut to make. A warning.

She had handled herself like a pro and that fact was the only thing that caused him to doubt her innocence. Still, would a professional killer be trusting enough to fall asleep in the presence of a perfect stranger? It wasn't something he would ever do. "Come on, sweetheart, let's go."

Laurie jerked awake. "What's wrong?"

"I'm finished. We need to get you home." He busied himself picking up the used gauze and paper.

Laurie absently traced the sticky edge of the tape and adjusted her clothes. She watched his long fingers quickly repack the kit and latch the hook. "Guess it wasn't too bad."

"Naw, just a nick really." J.D. slid the case back under the couch on the far wall and picked up her coat. "He must have heard me coming and split."

"I suppose. Although I don't think he really meant to hurt me."

J.D. frowned at her. "What do you mean by that? The guy came at you with a knife, didn't he?"

Laurie shrugged and winced as the movement tugged at her wound. "I think he had me mixed up with someone else. I think it was about drugs."

J.D. stood patiently, waiting for her to continue. This was totally out of character.

"He said he was delivering a message. Something about a package that 'they' wanted back."

"A package? Did he say what was in the package?" J.D. held up her coat for her.

"No, just that they would be contacting me again." Laurie slipped into the coat grinning. "Someone has trained you well."

"My granny. My folks were killed when I was thirteen and my grandparents raised me and my little sister, Katie." J.D. knew that this piece of information was one of the reasons he had been chosen to trap Laurie. Her file had informed him that her parents had been killed by a terrorist's bomb five years ago. Clifton hoped that having this morbid fact in common might cause Laurie to be more accepting of J.D. Personally, J.D. thought that was a load of crap. If Laurie was as sharp as Clifton made her out to be, she would be suspicious of everyone. A woman didn't go around killing terrorists to avenge her parents' deaths without developing a "little voice" of her own.

"I'm sorry." J.D. looked in her eyes and knew she meant it.

"Thanks." He cleared his throat and led her from the building. "You said the guy threatened to come back. Did he say when?"

"No. I hope he'll realize he's got the wrong woman." She wrapped her scarf around her neck as they slid onto the ice covered parking lot. "Anyway, I hope the police can catch him before he can hurt someone."

"A little late for that." J.D. held her arm as they shuffled to his Bronco. "I think you'd better be extra careful for a while just in case he comes back."

"If he comes back, he'll wish he hadn't."

J.D. heard the determination in her voice. He got the feeling that Ms. Laurie Morrison could probably take care of herself.

They sat in silence while the Bronco warmed up. Laurie sat stiffly on her side of the vehicle, her hands clenched tightly in her lap. "You want to go home or to the police station?"

"Home, please. My sister is probably worried about me."

"With good reason, I would say. What were you doing at the mall tonight anyway? I thought everyone went home early today." He cursed himself for the lie. He had been aware of every move she had made today and been hot on her trail, except for a few minutes. The minutes when she had been accosted by the "slasher." Damn!

"I stayed to catch up on some paperwork. We've

only got a week until the Christmas season starts. Everyone is working overtime."

J.D. eased the Bronco into gear and miraculously steered it in a straight path across the ice. "Directions?"

His gentle tone made it impossible to be affronted by the command. "South on Western."

He pressed on the gas pedal and the tires spun seeking traction on the glassy street. The Bronco swerved and Laurie clenched her seat belt. J.D. bit off a grin when he noticed her foot pressing an imaginary brake pedal. Here was a woman who didn't relinquish control easily.

Deftly steering against the slide, J.D. brought them under control. Following her quietly spoken directions, J.D. drove them through the slick streets. A couple of times he had been afraid they would end up in somebody's front lawn but they finally pulled up in front of an impressive two-story home. The gingerbread trim and window shutters of the Victorian structure were a gleaming white against the deep blue clapboards. When he had checked out her address earlier, he had been surprised. For some reason he had pictured this suspected terrorist in ultra modern chrome and glass. Even a few of those abstract paintings thrown in to cater to her pretentious nature. He allowed a low whistle of appreciation and Laurie turned to smile at him.

"It's great, isn't it? My parents spent years restoring it."

J.D. thought again how different she was from his expectations. According to what Clifton had told him, she was a man-eater. Had even slept with a few of her intended victims. The woman sitting next to him was either a very experienced manipulator or a saint. J.D. had never considered himself a religious man. Until lately.

"I guess I better go. Thanks again for all your help."

"Hold on a second." J.D. leaned over and engulfed her hand in his. "Are you gonna be okay? I can come in and stay for a while if you want. At least until the cops get here."

"That's nice, but I'll be fine. Pitsie's here and I'll be sure to lock all the doors." She fumbled with her seat belt. With his eyes on her, she felt like a microscopic germ under a microscope. His eyes had watched every move she made all night. She felt uneasy under that blue gaze. Uneasy and incredibly attracted.

He held her hand as she gingerly stepped down from the Bronco. Only when he felt she had her footing did he let go. The separation was so sudden that Laurie turned too quickly and felt her feet slide out from under her. Still in a daze from the unusual attraction to J.D., her reflexes were hazy and she groped helplessly for something to steady her. Nothing!

She heard her breath swoosh out as her body came in contact with the ice-covered curb. Her head hit the corner of the door and J.D.'s startled expression was the last thing she saw before disappearing under the chassis of the car.

These things really do happen in slow motion, he thought, as he watched Laurie slip and twist in front of him. The look on her face would have been funny if he hadn't been so scared. In an instant he was out of the car, completely forgetting the ice in his concern for Laurie. The second his boots hit the glazed street, he realized he had made a tactical error. Grasping the side of the Bronco for support, his gloved hand merely slid down the side. In a split second, he was flat on his back.

"Oh my gosh, are you okay?" Laurie asked from under the Bronco.

"Hell yes! Got a wonderful view from here." J.D. was so mad at his own stupidity that it took him a minute to realize Laurie was laughing. "Glad you think this is so dad-burned funny."

"I'm sorry, but I can't help it," she sputtered between giggles. "We look so funny."

J.D. had to admit they did look rather odd. Allowing a grin to soften his hard features, he carefully rolled onto his stomach and peered under the car. "I've had women try to get me flat on my back before, but this is a new twist."

"Never let it be said that Laurie Morrison does anything the easy way."

J.D. was a little surprised by her attitude. Instead of crying or screeching, she scooted over to his side of the Bronco and began crawling up beside him. "Do you think you could help me up? I think I twisted my ankle." Laurie knelt over him and brushed an errant lock of chocolate colored hair out of his eyes.

"Why didn't you say something!"

"I just did." Laurie sat on her rear end and glared at him. "You weren't exactly in any position to help me before."

Irritated that she had reminded him of his fall from grace, J.D. slid his hands carefully up the car and regained his balance before stooping to help Laurie to her feet. "Which ankle?"

"The right one, I think." Laurie grunted as he reached under her arms and hoisted her to her feet.

"You think? You mean you don't know your right foot from your left?" J.D. tried sarcasm to quell the tidal wave of heat she had set loose in his loins. Her hair spread across the broad expanse of his chest like a fragrant fan. The softness of her well wrapped body crushed very nicely into his.

"No, silly. I mean they both hurt. I think the left one is just stunned, but the right one is really throbbing."

It's not the only thing that's throbbing, J.D. thought.

He quickly bent and scooped her into his arms. Even wrapped as she was, he held her easily against him. She facilitated the hold by clasping her arms around his neck, bringing them face to face. "Do you think this is necessary?" The small puffs of frozen breath twirled in his face.

"It'll be easier for me to break your fall if you land on me." Dumb excuse for holding a woman, J.D. chided. Not that he'd ever needed an excuse before. Most women more than threw themselves into his arms. Women were becoming a heck of a lot more aggressive and J.D. had become rather adept at playing defense.

Laurie was close enough to feel the heat of his cheek on hers. She found she enjoyed being on the same level with a man. At her height it was rare that she was able to comfortably look into a man's eyes. She had never known a man to sweep her off her feet. Literally or figuratively. His face didn't even show the strain of her weight. She abhorred the fact that she was a good fifteen pounds overweight and realized that if most of her dates tried picking her up, they would end up in traction. Too bad, this was certainly a turn-on.

J.D. carefully made his way to the front porch, walking across the grass rather than the sidewalk. The frozen earth crackled beneath his feet and he tried to concentrate on where he was stepping. The porch had been heavily sanded and he sent up a prayer of thanks for the traction. "Do you have your key?"

"Just ring the . . ." Laurie's voice drifted away when J.D. turned to face her. Their noses almost touched. Laurie couldn't seem to form coherent thoughts under his electric gaze. "I don't understand," she whispered, tightening her hold on his neck as she brought her lips to his.

"Aw, sweetheart." He groaned against her mouth. Calling himself every kind of a fool, he gave in to her.

He shifted her in his arms to acquaint himself better with the feel of her body. The friction of her sliding against him was his undoing. Groaning into her mouth, he fell back against the door frame. Her lips were so sweet and soft, yet they were demanding more from him than he intended to give. Her fingers curled in his hair so tightly he thought she might yank it out. Oddly enough, he couldn't have cared less. She could have snatched him bald as long as she didn't deprive him of her lips.

Heat coursed through Laurie, yet she shivered. Her mind was a blank. Every nerve ending in her body seemed connected to her lips. She felt the kiss clear to her toes. The thought that they might freeze together flickered through her mind. She couldn't be so lucky.

"Whoa!" Pitsie's shout pierced her almost pornographic thoughts and she pulled herself from J.D.

J.D. blinked against the sudden light from the porch overhead. Laurie's face was flushed bright red. The heat in her eyes told him that the glow she was sporting had nothing to do with the weather.

"Man, Laurie! I've been worried sick about you and you've been making out on the front porch."

J.D. grinned at the young girl standing in the doorway. A smaller, blonder version of the woman he held in his arms, he decided she must be the little sister he had read about in the files.

"Uh, don't be silly. We were just . . . uh . . . just. Just what were we doing?" Laurie pleaded with her eyes.

"Making out."

THREE

Laurie snuggled deeper into her pillow, seeking a few more minutes of sleep. Her ankle was sore and swallowing sent streaks of pain shooting through her jaw. The tape on her neck tugged at her skin and she reached up to pick at the curled up edge. When J.D. had carried her to the bedroom last night, Pitsie had burst into tears. Too late, Laurie realized how scary she must look.

J.D. had taken a few minutes to calm Pitsie's fears and steer her toward the kitchen for some ice and aspirin. While she was gone he took the opportunity to press his lips to hers for a brief kiss. "I don't know about you, but I haven't been caught necking on the front porch for more than a decade."

"I don't even remember necking on the front porch," she giggled.

J.D.'s eyebrows shot up. "What was wrong with you? Didn't you like necking?"

He clasped Laurie tighter with his left arm and reached down to fling back her bedspread. She clung to him as he lowered her to the crisp clean rose-colored sheets. His face was a mask of composure but Laurie felt his pulse racing before he released her. The knowledge that he was as affected by their extraordinary attraction to one another as she was, provided small comfort. She often found herself in the clutches of some man whose libido automatically disconnected his brain. In those times she was almost grateful for her inability to become passionate. Time and again, her clear head and lack of emotional response had enabled her to defuse a potentially embarrassing situation with only a modicum of discomfort for either party. Now, when she desperately needed it, her unflappable composure had flown the coop.

Pitsie and J.D. had tried to convince her to go to the hospital for X-rays, but she had stubbornly refused. She hadn't been able to dissuade him from staying and helping Pitsie fix her a light supper, though. She had refrained from commenting on the fact that he had eaten more than half of the food on her tray while trying to convince her to eat. Before he left he had telephoned the police about the attack, checked every lock in the house, and propped her foot up so high she felt like a Rockette.

Pitsie had been totally enamoured of J.D. from the moment he had stepped over the threshold with Laurie. If Laurie hadn't been suffering from the same malady, she would have found Pitsie's adoration sweet. As it was, she prayed her eyes didn't shine quite so obviously. What was it about the man that snuck past all her carefully constructed barricades? How did his particular brand of charm succeed where so many others had failed?

Laurie felt the rhythmic beat of Pitsie's stereo pounding upstairs. J.D. had commented on the way Pitsie had handled the entire situation last night. Once he had assured her that Laurie was safe and relatively unharmed, she had calmly accepted his explanation of the wild events surrounding the evening. Only a slight chuckle had escaped when he got to the part about falling on the ice.

Laurie had to admit J.D.'s explanation of the night's activities sounded a bit far-fetched, but Pitsie seemed to take it all at face value. For that Laurie was eternally grateful. Lately, she never knew where she stood with the seventeen year old. Laurie didn't exactly remember when Pitsie's mood swings had started, but she was definitely ready for them to stop. She had suspected the girl was experimenting with drugs at first and it had scared Laurie to death. Drugs didn't seem to be the problem, though. Whatever was bothering Pitsie was evidently a personal matter, one she wasn't ready to share with her older sister. Laurie tried to remember what she had been like as a teenager, but she didn't recall ever acting like Pitsie was. Of course, at seventeen she had been suffering from tunnel-vision. All her time and energy had been spent preparing for a Naval career.

Seventeen was a lifetime ago. A distant memory, untouched by deceit, pain, and death. Tears welled up in Laurie's eyes and she wiped them away with the back of her hand. She hadn't felt the need to reminisce in a very long time. The desire to crawl back under the covers and wallow in self-pity was strong. Laurie bolted out of the bed before she succumbed to temptation.

Her ankle protested the sudden weight and she clenched her teeth to keep from crying out. Not that Pitsie would hear her over the noise blaring down the stairs, but Laurie prided herself on staying in complete control. At all times.

She preferred not to think about how out of control J.D. had made her feel last night. The only conciliation was that J.D. hadn't possessed any more control than she had. She had felt his breath quicken every time she touched him. Having the power to cause a man like J.D. to become slightly unhinged was exhilarating.

She heard Pitsie storm down the stairs and decided it was safe to run her bath water. When her dad had redone the plumbing, he had neglected to take into consideration the amount of hot water two women could use.

She managed to hobble to her bathroom and shut the door against interruptions. She hadn't even taken her make-up off last night. Clogging pores had been the least of her concerns. Thank goodness this was Saturday and she could indulge in a leisurely bath instead of a quick shower.

The downstairs bed and bath had been her parents. After they were killed and Laurie had returned home to finish raising her brother and sister, she had decided to use it. The bathroom held a treasure chest of memories. She had helped her mother scour every antique store in the tri-state area. Her mom had had very specific ideas on how she wanted her home decorated. Countless auctions and estate sales had provided the antique claw-footed tub and pedestal sink.

In fact, most of the house was furnished with antiques that her parents had found during her dad's Navy career. When they had returned to Amarillo, her dad had spent several years restoring the old Victorian-style house. Laurie hadn't changed much in the house in the last five years. The bathroom was one room that she had left alone. Laura Ashley prints in teal and rose decorated the walls and framed the stain-glass window. Pitsie had redone the bath upstairs after Bubba had left for basic training, but Laurie had never considered changing anything that her mother had done.

She perched on the edge of the tub and began filling it with hot water. A few scoops of bath salts made the room smell divine. The window fogged up nicely and

Laurie carefully lowered herself into the too hot water. Her bottom protested the heat and she squealed.

No sooner had she let loose with her primal yell than the bathroom door was flung open. J.D. stood in the doorway with a maniacal look on his face.

It took a minute for J.D. to register the fact that Laurie wasn't hurt. All he could assimilate was the fact that she was naked. Beautifully naked. The water in the tub was a purple color and her full breasts swayed with the gentle flow of the water. As soon as she recovered, she wrapped her arms tightly around her. "Can I help you?"

Yes, move your arms, he wanted to shout. Instead, he stammered something he hoped was appropriate and backed out of the room. He reached up and ran a hand over his face. He was sweating, but he didn't know if it was due to the heat in the bathroom or the heat running through him.

Man, she was a cool one. She hadn't screamed or fainted. She hadn't even jerked one of those funny colored towels around her. He knew for sure that he wouldn't have been so calm if she had barged in on him buck naked.

"Stupid cowboy. Was he raised in a barn?" Laurie muttered quietly to herself as she dried off and stepped into her robe. She tried to maintain her fury, but when she thought of his face, she couldn't. He had obviously decided she was hurt when she yelled and he had been rushing to her rescue.

J.D. sat on the couch and played with the cup in his hands. How sad to see a brilliant career end like this. For years he had been able to ferret out even the most cunning criminals. He alone had been responsible for the nation's security on more than one occasion, and he succeeded where everyone else had failed. Foreign dignitaries had asked for him personally. Even during his semi-retirement, he had helped his fellow agents with his analytical brain-power. Now, it was only a fond memory. One tiny redhead with a freckle on her breast had done what no one else had ever been able to accomplish. She had rendered him impotent as an agent. If Laurie Morrison really was the head of an international terrorist organization, she was safe from him.

Laurie emerged from the bathroom. J.D. looked out of place on the red velvet sofa. His large hands engulfed the fine bone china cup. He glanced up from his cup and managed a half-smirk. She could read the confusion in his eyes.

"I see you've made yourself at home." Laurie picked up a second cup of coffee from the inlaid coffee table. "At least Pitsie remembered her manners."

"She seemed to think I'd be welcome." He peered at her over the rim of his cup. "I hope she was right."

"In my house, yes. In my bathroom . . . not without an invitation." Her right eyebrow raised to punctuate her meaning.

"How do you do that?" J.D. asked, indicating her eyebrow.

"I don't know. I can cross one eye, too." Laurie shrugged. The abrupt change of topic threw her from offense to defense. The man evidently liked being in control. She couldn't blame him, it was a position she also preferred.

J.D. grinned and couldn't think of anything else to say. He knew it was his turn, but his mind was still mulling over the way she had looked in the bathtub. He longed to take her back in there and show her what those oversize tubs were for. The thought of having her under him, writhing in purple water pleased him immensely.

Laurie liked the look in his eyes. "Are you here for a reason?"

J.D.'s mind was still in the bathtub and she had to ask him twice before he heard her. "I talked with the police again this morning and they wondered if you felt like comin' in yet. They wanted to see you last night but I told 'em to forget it."

"You what!" Laurie leapt to her feet. A shooting pain in her ankle forced her to sit back down. "How dare you answer for me!"

"Sit down!" J.D. angrily crossed the room and sat down next to her, lifting her foot onto his lap. "I told them what had happened, and gave them the description you gave me. I told the sergeant you were worn out and he said we could wait until this morning."

"I knew I should have talked with them myself." She tried to ignore the sensations his hands were creating as he gently massaged her foot. She had always heard the feet could be erogenous zones but she had never expected to have such a kinky fetish herself. "Maybe they could have caught the man."

"Now, darlin', you don't really believe that." J.D. heard the moan echoing in her head and slowly slid his hands up her calf. "You're just mad 'cause I didn't tell you about it."

Laurie's head fell back on the couch and she closed her eyes. "Well, maybe. But I don't like people trying to control my life."

"I'm sorry, okay? I just didn't think you could handle any more last night." He reached down and lifted her other foot onto his lap. He was fascinated by the fact that she didn't have a toenail on her little toe. The rest of her toenails were painted a bright red. He wiggled each toe, mentally reciting "this little piggy."

"What are you doing?"

J.D.'s head snapped up and he noticed Laurie had sat

up. "Playing this little piggy with the cutest little piggies I've ever seen."

"Oh gross!"

Laurie swiveled around to stare at Pitsie. "When did you come in?"

"This little piggy went to market, I think." Pitsie flopped down in the chair across from Laurie and J.D. "Don't you think that's kinda stupid?"

J.D. wiggled Laurie's toes again. "Nope. Actually I thought it was kinda fun."

"Would you two hush." Laurie retracted her feet from J.D. and slid them up under her long velour robe. "What time did the police say to come in?"

J.D. recognized a "let's keep this strictly business" voice when he heard one. "I told him we'd be there before noon so you'd better get hoppin'."

"*We'd* be there?"

"You can't drive, remember." J.D. patted her foot through the protection of her robe. "Besides, I was the hero. Maybe they'll give me a medal."

"Oh, brother." Laurie stood up carefully. The last thing she needed right now was to fall on her face and have J.D. touch her again. Just being in the same room with him was playing havoc with her senses. When he touched her they sent her mind into a chaotic state she had never experienced before. She had no defense against the mindless sensuality he caused.

"Need any help dressing?"

Laurie glared at him for a second before shutting the bathroom door sharply. She could hear Pitsie giggling through the thick oak door. She had to be very careful how she handled this . . . whatever it was she felt for J.D. She had always been open with Pitsie about sex and men and dating. Or at least she thought she had. If all women turned into a mindless glob of jelly when they were attracted to a man, it was no wonder men dominated the world. How could a woman even hope to defend herself against a man that could make her feel like J.D. made her feel? She shuddered to think about Pitsie experiencing this kind of passion at her age. No wonder teenage boys thought about sex all the time. Hormones were nasty little things.

She slipped on a pair of hot pink silk panties and matching bra. Her jeans were a bit tricky considering how tight they were. She stretched across her bed and held her breath until the zipper was up. The seat of her pants was alarmingly tight, but thankfully her sweater almost reached her knees.

She deftly applied her make-up. Her pale complexion was a gray pasty color this morning and she went a little heavy on the blush. The cut on her neck had already begun to form a scab and she fished a bandage out of the medicine cabinet to cover it. The v-neck of her sweater hid all but the corner of the bandage, but hopefully no one would notice.

"You gonna take all day?" J.D. pounded on the bathroom door and Laurie sprayed perfume in her eyes.

Grabbing a wash cloth she quickly stopped the burning, reconsidering her position on profanity. There were times when "pooh" just didn't cut it. "I'm coming, hold your horses."

J.D. mumbled something unintelligible and Laurie heard him pacing the hallway. She hadn't taken that long and she resented the fact that he was hurrying her.

" 'Bout time." J.D. was standing by the front door holding her coat.

"Oh hush." She slipped into the coat and his arms. "I didn't take that long."

J.D. held her longer than necessary but neither one seemed to mind. "I guess I just want to get this over with. I keep thinking about what he said."

"About coming back?"

J.D. nodded as he helped her into his Bronco. "What if he doesn't figure out that you're the wrong lady?"

"I don't want to think about it."

J.D. growled. "Honey, you might not have any choice."

He slammed her door shut and went around to his side. Laurie knew he was right. She did have to think about what the man wanted and why he thought she had it.

The ride to the police station was strained and Laurie was relieved when they were finally led into Detective Anderson's office.

"Have a seat, folks." He was a large man with a few strands of hair wrapped around his head in an attempt to cover his scalp. His desk was covered with papers and napkins from fast food places. "Want some coffee?"

"No, thank you. I'd just like to get this over with." Laurie sat in the chair J.D. held for her. He slid another chair next to her and reached over to take her hand. Part of her wanted to snatch it from his grasp, keep him at a distance. The other part was glad for the comfort and support. She entangled her fingers with his.

"From this report I'm afraid there's not much we can do." The detective held a report in one hand and a coffee cup in the other.

"What do you mean, nothing you can do?" Laurie leaned forward. "I was attacked and could have been seriously injured."

J.D. clenched her fingers in a sympathetic rhythm. "I think what he means is there's just not a whole lot to go on."

"That's right, Miss Morrison. You didn't see his face did you?"

Laurie shook her head. Logically she realized that the detective was right. She couldn't give the police any kind of a description. She knew the procedures. The questions to be asked. The odds against catching a criminal with a perfect description were high. Without a description they were astronomical.

"Don't suppose you remembered anything else?" The detective reached into a paper sack and produced a breakfast sandwich. "Want one?"

"Detective, I came here to catch a criminal, not eat brunch."

J.D. unwrapped their fingers and slid his arm around her shoulders pulling her back in her chair. "Laurie, sweetheart, calm down. The detective was just bein' nice. He knows what we're here for."

Laurie wanted to smash something, anything, over J.D.'s head right then. "I don't remember anything else. Just some nut wanting a package."

The detective had put down his coffee and sandwich. He was first and foremost a police officer and he didn't want to offend the beautiful young woman sitting across from him. The police had enough trouble instilling confidence in the public's mind without aggravating them. "Ms. Morrison, I assure you we will do everything we can to catch the man. You just haven't given us much to go on. Do you have any idea what package he was talking about?"

"No. The only thing I could come up with was a drug transfer."

The detective nodded his head and the overhead light played on the exposed skin of his scalp. "That's as good a guess as any. Being on two major interstate highways like we are, drug trafficking is a major problem. Could be the mall is a regular drop site."

"That's impossible." Laurie shook her head vigorously. "There is no way that something like that could go on without my being aware of it."

The detective opened his mouth to say something, but thought better of it. "Well, I'm going to put a couple of undercover men in the vicinity just to be sure."

"Do you really think someone in the mall could be dealing in drugs?" Laurie thought of the merchants and the elderly people she talked with everyday.

"Ms. Morrison, you'd be surprised at the people involved with drugs. There's just too much money to be made. We can't convince the pushers to give up several hundred thousand dollars a year for a respectable job making minimum wage."

Laurie nodded her head in agreement and they concluded their business. J.D. had assured the detective that he would personally see to her safety. Laurie tried not to blush at the quizzical look the man shot in their direction. She was well aware of the implication of such a statement. J.D. was effectively staking his claim. A man taking care of his woman. Lord, but she liked the feeling of being his woman. Intellectually, she had trouble with the notion. She felt sure J.D. would work his way around her logic.

"How 'bout grabbing a bite to eat?"

"J.D., I appreciate everything you've done, but frankly I'm just worn out."

"Guess you just want to go home, huh?"

"Mmmm." Laurie laid her head on the back of the seat and relaxed as J.D. maneuvered in and out of traffic. By the time he pulled up in front of her house, she was asleep.

"You sure do things to a guy's ego," he whispered in her ear. Since she didn't pull away, he took the chance to nibble on her ear lobe.

"Cut that out." Laurie reached up and playfully swatted at him. "Boy, you never stop, do you?"

"Not if I can help it." He made another pass at her neck and she hopped out of the Bronco. "Whoa, there, wait for me."

Laurie mumbled something about not being a horse, but she waited for him to walk her to the front door anyway. He might be a lech but she couldn't fault his manners. She'd be willing to bet he had never honked for a date in his life. She could still hear her dad chewing out Billy Wilson for not coming to the door to pick up his daughter. Laurie had been moritified, but Billy never honked his horn in front of her house again.

"Well, you've seen me safely to my door. Your duty is done." She held out her hand to him.

J.D. looked at her offer and chuckled. "Little late for that, don't you think?" He placed a large hand on both of her shoulders and quickly kissed her slightly parted lips. His tongue briefly flicked over her full bottom lip. Laurie opened her lips to give him entrance but he stood up and left her gaping. He placed a finger under her chin and gently closed her lips. "Next time, darlin'."

Laurie watched until his Bronco turned the corner before entering the house. She would need the rest of the day to come to some conclusion about her behavior. She was seriously afraid she had lost her mind.

J.D. was grateful for the hazardous road conditions. They commanded his complete attention. Once he was at his apartment, however, there was nothing to keep him from thinking about Laurie and the strange power she seemed to have over him.

Funny how he had thought he had known everything about her. Whoever had prepared her file had failed to mention that she was a remarkably nice woman. He had expected a worldly career woman. Someone who knew the game and how it was played. A woman he could imagine slitting the throat of an enemy. He couldn't even imagine Laurie carving a turkey.

He had roamed the mall freely last night looking for evidence. Clifton had secured a position as the security guard for him and he planned on using it to his advantage. He had taken his time, thoroughly searching the mall. The locks on her desk had been much too easy to pick. A quick shuffle through her papers told him exactly what he had expected. Nothing. He had combed her office to no avail. Rather than prove her innocence, it helped build the case against her. If she were the professional Clifton suspected, she wouldn't leave anything in her desk. Her house either for that matter. He knew getting better acquainted with her was the only way to prove her innocence. Or guilt.

When he laid the facts out in front of him, he had to admit Clifton had just cause for his suspicions. For the past three years a small group of expert assassins had begun ridding the world of some of its more unsavory characters. Clifton claimed that Laurie was the top dog. She determined who, where, when, and how. The why was easy. Five years ago her parents had been the innocent victims of a car bombing. Some fanatical religious group claimed responsibility. Their leader had been the first to die. J.D. had to admire the way each execution went off. More than thirty known terrorists and war criminals had been expertly killed. In all of the executions not one innocent bystander had died. Laurie and her morbid band of merry men were indeed killing the scum to protect the innocent. J.D. suspected Clifton was mad because Laurie's group was doing a better job than TAT.

J.D. read the cold hard facts over again, trying to find a clue that would link this mystery terrorists-hater to the woman who had fallen asleep on him. Twice!

FOUR

Laurie checked her reflection in the mirror one more time. She couldn't remember ever being this nervous before a date.

J.D. had shown up at the mall this morning to help with the Christmas decorations. They had passed the morning in harmony, so when he asked her to dinner, she said yes. Frankie had teased her mercilessly as usual.

To top it off, J.D. had sent her a bouquet of flowers from the flower shop in the mall, so by late afternoon the entire mall knew about the date.

One of the mall walkers, Henry Greenhaw, had sat her down and quietly inquired how much she really knew about "her new young man." She had made light of Henry's grandfatherly concern, but the question was a valid one. She didn't know anything about J.D. other than the obvious. Great body, great eyes, great hair, and great lips.

Luckily, Henry was too caught up in romancing one of the new lady walkers to get too involved in her love life. Laurie had noticed the dark-haired woman a few days ago, after Henry had pointed her out. Her name was Margaret Washburn and Laurie couldn't get over the feeling she had met the woman somewhere.

Unfortunately, Margaret had taken an instant dislike to Laurie and all of Laurie's attempts at friendliness had been rebuked.

Although Laurie didn't exactly approve of Henry's courtship of Margaret, she was grateful that it kept him out of her social life.

Laurie grabbed an emery board and flicked it over her newly filed fingernails. She had broken two nails this afternoon helping Frankie with the Christmas decorations. The decorations had to be up before Santa arrived on Friday and since no one wanted to work on Thanksgiving, everyone was working overtime.

Although she had been thankful for J.D.'s assistance with the crates this morning, she had been surprised that he had taken such an active interest in the mall. None of the previous guards had ever shown up when they were off duty. Laurie wondered if he was attracted to her or the thought of catching a horde of drug dealers.

The doorbell rang just as Laurie was buckling the strap of her shoe. Pitsie stormed down the stairs to answer it, so Laurie took a few minutes to play with the cawl collar of her emerald green sweater dress. She tried to decide on the perfect greeting.

"Why, J.D., don't you look nice." She grinned at her green eyed reflection and shook her head. No, that was stupid.

Come on Laurie, be brilliant, witty, sultry. "J.D., I can't tell you how I've looked forward to this evening." She tried lowering her voice and batting her eyelashes. Ugh, that sounded like something off the late, late, late show.

Checking the line of her dress one more time she opened the door and tried walking without tripping. She hadn't felt this giddy when she was a teenager. She had been out with men from every corner of the world and all walks of life. J.D. should have been a walk in the park. Except that it was Central Park in the dead of night. Eerie, exciting, and altogether not the thing to do.

J.D. was sitting on the couch facing her. When she entered the room, he stood up. He was wearing brand new starched jeans and a blue and white striped shirt that just matched his eyes. The ends of his hair curled slightly and she noticed they were damp. Damp hair brought to mind J.D. in a shower. Stop it, girl, that line of thinking will get you in trouble!

J.D. wanted to cry when she held up her coat for him to hold. It was a sin to cover up that body. He hoped he didn't end up making a fool of himself. He was already debating whether or not she was wearing a bra. The top of her dress was off her shoulders and the tiny buttons up the front wouldn't be much of a challenge. The material was some kind of soft clingy stuff that grabbed her the way he wanted to. He didn't allow himself to watch her walk toward the car.

The restaurant was one of Laurie's favorites and she was delighted when J.D. ordered lobster for them. He sat across from her and his long legs occasionally brushed against hers.

Though he made polite conversation, he kept staring at her neck and she began to panic. Did she have a bug crawling down her neck? She reached up and ran her hand down the delicate column of her throat. Nothing felt wrong. Maybe it was her dress. He had seemed to like it earlier, but maybe he felt it was too much. Too low? Too tight? Why was he staring at her like that? He was driving her crazy!

Lord, she is driving me crazy! Why is she twitching like that? Doesn't she know that dress is almost falling off? J.D. shifted in his seat trying to get comfortable. Of course, she knows what she's doing, you idiot! She's a professional.

They lapsed into an uncomfortable silence and J.D. knew he had her worried. Thank goodness for years of training. They were the edge he needed to keep fully aware of her as an agent rather than a woman.

According to Clifton the organization Laurie headed was basically a terrorist-for-hire type. Like so many others that had started out to stop terrorism for the best of reasons, they had succumbed to the monetary temptation. The group was international, selective, and very expensive. They had recruited top assassins from all nations. Each hit was so carefully planned and executed that there had never been an accident. No car bombs to kill innocent bystanders, no gangland-style slayings with machine guns blazing in the darkness. Clifton swore all their information pointed to Laurie. He had been so confident that a little in-depth surveillance was all that was required to snare the lovely lady in her own web of duplicity. J.D. had forgotten Clifton's gift of understatement. In J.D.'s world nothing was ever simple.

"Would you like to go dancing or maybe catch a movie?" He knew all she wanted to do was go home, but he needed to keep her off balance if he wanted her to slip up.

"I'm really tired, J.D. I think I should just go home."

The ride to her house was as silent as the dinner and Laurie was tempted to scream just to relieve the tension. "I'm not sure what went wrong tonight, but thanks for the dinner."

"I didn't realize there was anything wrong." J.D. held her hand on the seat between them so she couldn't make a run for it. The confusion in her eyes told him that his switch in tactics had had the desired effect.

Laurie noticed the house was dark and glanced at her

watch. Only nine-thirty and Pitsie was already asleep. Odd. But then everything Pitsie did lately was odd.

"Can I come in for a little while?" His hand tightened on hers. "Please?"

The porch light was the only light and J.D. quickly stepped in front of Laurie to find the inside light switch. "You should tell Pitsie to leave a light on until you get home."

"She usually does." Laurie took his coat and nestled it onto the hook next to hers. "Would you care for tea or something stronger? I think there's some wine in this cabinet."

Laurie bent over and began shuffling through the bottles in the lower cabinet of the hutch. Did she have any idea what the sight of her bent over in that dress did to a man? A groan escaped him and he quickly converted it into a cough.

"Are you okay? You're not catching a cold are you?" Laurie straightened and pressed her hand to his face. Her fingers were warm against his cool cheek. He slowly turned his head and pressed his lips to the palm of her hand. His tongue crept out to brand a pattern on her. This time the groan was hers and she made no effort to disguise it. Her lips parted and her tongue traced the fullness of her lower lip. Her breath came in spurts and she felt a brief surge of panic. It was gone as quickly as it had flared. Instinctively she knew that this man would be patient and gentle. He would be the one to help her overcome the horrifying memories that haunted her.

J.D. tugged her closer and she fell against him. His breath fanned her lips as he lowered his head to her. She arched up to meet him. Her hand slid from his cheek to the back of his head and she held him to her. His tongue darted over her lips and retreated. His pace was slow and gentle, giving her time to encourage or pull away. Her stomach quivered as his lips left hers to seek the sweetness of her neck. The open collar of the dress gave him free access to her shoulders and the oh-so-sensitive area behind her ears. Her hand clenched the front of his shirt, her nails digging impatiently into his chest.

"This isn't gonna work, darlin'." His voice was a soft rumble in her ear. What was wrong now? Didn't he like it? How could he not be even a little moved by the hurricane of emotion whipping through her. "Do you think we might move over to the couch while I can still walk?"

Laurie stared up at him and without waiting for an answer, he lifted her off her feet and crossed the room. Settling her on his lap, she found solid evidence of just how affected he was. She tried an experimental wiggle and was rewarded with the sexiest moan she had ever heard.

J.D. resumed their kiss and this time Laurie could feel his heart pounding under her hand. Though he was infinitely tender, she could sense the urgency. His lips took what hers freely gave. His hands caressed her and she could feel his fingers tremble. Moving back from him, she looked into his eyes and found her passion mirrored there. Just knowing she could stop him gave her the courage to continue. Her need was too great. His eyes were too blue and filled with promises he didn't realize he was offering.

"Laurie? Babe, it's up to you. I don't mean to rush you, but I can't seem to help myself. If you want me to go I will. Not happily you understand, but I'll go."

Laurie was unsure of her voice. "It's not a matter of wanting, J.D. If that was all there was to it, I would have thrown you down among the various reindeer parts this morning. But, well . . ." She let out the breath she had been holding and J.D. heard her regret.

"It's okay, I know it's too soon." He shifted her off his lap, but he kept his arms wrapped tightly around her. It would take a few minutes before he could comfortably stand up.

"No, it's not that. Well, not entirely. It is too soon, I guess. Hoo boy, I've never had this much trouble before." She tested a small grin in his direction and was rewarded with a similar pained expression.

"I'm not sure how to take that. Are you having trouble turning me down, or with the thought of our making love?" His arm crept back around her.

The fact that he considered it making love brought another smile to her lips, this one more natural. "J.D., I have never had trouble turning any man down before, but I am having some trouble with the thought of our becoming intimate." Laurie saw the hurt in his eyes and rushed ahead to reassure him. "No, J.D., it's not that I don't trust you. I do. I don't know why, but I do. I know you wouldn't hurt me. It's just, well for one thing there's Pitsie."

J.D. closed his eyes. "Sweetheart, I'm sorry. I completely forgot about her. Hell, I could kick myself for putting you in this position. We could have gone to my place."

"It's nice of you to offer your place for our illicit rendezvous, but that isn't all of it. You see, I'm not sure how to handle this situation."

"Just what is the situation?" Doubt had brought a harsh note back to his voice. Laurie felt his arms slacken.

"I'm making such a mess of this. I suppose the best thing would be to tell you straight out. I'm a little scared of how you'll react."

J.D. suddenly remembered who he was dealing with. During the last few minutes, Laurie had gone from being the enemy to something much more than a friend.

Now he looked deep into her eyes. Could they hold such deception? Man, he had really screwed up.

"What is it? I promise it won't matter." J.D. switched to his "charm them out of their pants" voice. Smooth, Westat, just get a confession and you'll have wrapped up this little assignment. No one has to know you tied it up with your heart.

"J.D., I've . . ." Laurie never finished the sentence. The crash of broken glass flying through the room sent J.D. sprawling across her.

"Stay down!" J.D. snarled and flew across the room toward a large chunk of black that had shattered the picture window.

"What is it?"

"Get away!" Panic ripped the words from him as he recognized the simple workings of a bomb. Scooping the offending package into his arms, he bolted for the back door. Leveling a kick at the knob, he splintered the lock and the door flew open. Tossing the package in the backyard, J.D. slid under the kitchen table.

"J.D.!" Laurie's scream echoed in the silence. Scrambling from her position on the floor, she ran through the kitchen and out the back door. She too had identified her surprise package and terror quivered in her stomach. Where was he?

Large hands caught her shoulders and she twirled to find her nose pressed to his chest. "I'm right here. It's okay."

She could hear her heart pounding in her ears. "What in the world is going on?" Her voice sounded brittle. "Pitsie!"

Tearing herself from J.D.'s grasp she sprinted toward the house and up the stairs. J.D. was on her heels trying to calm her. "I'm sure she's fine."

Thrusting Pitsie's door open she almost collapsed

with relief when she saw Pitsie in bed. "Thank goodness."

J.D. peered at the odd shaped lump in the bed and walked over to investigate.

"Don't wake her up," Laurie whispered.

"Not much chance of that." He yanked down the blanket to reveal a mass of stuffed animals.

"I don't believe it." Laurie sat on the edge of the bed and buried her face in her hands. "Just today she promised to act more mature."

"Aw, come on, Laurie, sneaking out to meet her boyfriend isn't that big a deal."

"Would you stay out of it?"

"Excuse me. I'll go call the police and tell them to send the bomb squad." He spun on his heel. "You have a much bigger problem to cope with. Your little sister is out having fun."

Raking her fingers through her hair she fought the urge to lay down and cry. Nothing had gone right tonight and it looked like it was going to get worse. Resigning herself to that fact, she plodded along after J.D.

The bitter wind was gleefully whipping through the gaping hole that had been a window. J.D.'s boots crunched on the scattered shards of glass. Laurie instinctively reached up and switched off the small lamp glowing in the corner of the living room.

"What did you do that for?" J.D. whispered.

"What are we whispering for?" she countered.

The room was dark but the street light provided enough light for him to see her eyes. What he saw there sent his heart plummeting. He saw her caution, her confusion, and most especially her anger. Everything but what he expected, no, wanted, to see there. Fear. Any normal woman would be terrified and hysterical. Hell, any man would be, too. Laurie had just had a bomb tossed through her window and except for her initial shakes, she was perfectly calm. She had turned out the light just as he was reaching for it. He hadn't wanted anyone who might be lurking outside to see in. Had the same thought occurred to her? Would it have occurred to anyone not trained to think in such a way? J.D. didn't want to know.

"I'll call the police." Laurie slipped past him to the kitchen and a few seconds later he heard her speaking to the police. The information she offered was clear and concise. Sounded like she was familiar with the routine.

A noise on the front porch grabbed his attention and his body went on alert. Someone was trying awfully hard not to make any noise and J.D. flattened himself against the wall by the front door. The lock jiggled and he cursed himself for not checking to make sure the door was locked. Raising his arms into an offensive stance, he prepared to give the intruder a pain in the neck.

The door opened only slightly and the intruder slipped inside, carefully closing the door without a sound. J.D. let loose with a war cry and wrapped his arms around . . . Pitsie!

"Let me go. Please let me go."

"Son of a . . ." J.D. dropped his arms and reached for the entry light.

Laurie came flying out of the kitchen. "What's the matter?"

"Look who's home, dear."

"Patsy Ann Morrison, where have you been?" Laurie was existing on an adrenalin high and her voice was high and piercing.

"I'm home before curfew."

J.D. took an arm of both women and led them toward Laurie's bedroom. "I think you need to figure out where you're gonna stay tonight before you do any sister squabbling."

Pitsie and Laurie both glared at him. He left them alone, deciding the bomb would probably be safer company at the moment. It was either a fake or on a timer so he didn't venture too close. He could hear Pitsie and Laurie talking rather vehemently behind the closed door. He wondered if Laurie noticed that Pitsie smelled like an ashtray. Whoever she had been with smoked and didn't shave close enough. He had noticed her neck and cheeks were bright red.

Laurie came out of the room and closed the door behind her. "She says she was out with Tiffanie, but she's lying. She smells like smoke and she's got a bad case of whisker burn."

"So I noticed. Don't be too hard on her, it's all part of growing up." J.D. pulled her in front of him and massaged her shoulders.

"Yeah? Well, learning to tell the truth is also part of it."

J.D.'s hands dropped and he walked away from Laurie. *Truth.*

FIVE

The snow plow had barely started on the parking lot by the time Laurie slid into her parking space. With any luck the weather would hold and the lot would be clear before the stores opened at ten. Thank goodness for the snow plow service the mall had under contract. That was one problem she wouldn't have to deal with this morning. Problems were not in short supply lately. She and J.D. had spent the wee hours of the morning dealing with the fire department, the bomb squad, and a very unpleasant Detective Anderson. J.D. had finally managed to convince Anderson that they had no idea what was going on.

J.D. had hauled the detective out to his car and had a private conversation with the man. Laurie didn't know what J.D. had told him, and frankly, she couldn't care less. All that mattered was Anderson had gotten into his car and gone away. Laurie realized that having a bomb tossed through her window two days after being attacked by a lunatic in the dead of night didn't improve her standing in the mind of the good detective, but she had told the truth. She had absolutely no idea what was going on.

J.D. had stuck with her throughout the myriad of stupid questions she had been required to answer. Pitsie had burst into tears at regular intervals and J.D. had finally persuaded Laurie to call someone to come and get the distraught girl.

Of course Pitsie had protested the idea of going to stay with Tiffanie, but in the end she saw the importance of getting out of the house. Someone believed that Laurie had something they wanted and until the police could find out who, neither of them was safe. Tiffanie's dad was a deputy sheriff and that fact alone lightened Laurie's burden.

Still Pitsie hadn't been happy. "I thought you said it was just a sick joke?"

"We're pretty sure it is, but I don't want to take any chances. Do you have any idea how hard it would be to replace a smart-mouthed seventeen year old?"

"Easy. All seventeen year olds are smart-mouthed."

Tiffanie's dad had promised to keep a close eye on Pitsie and Laurie had kissed her good-bye just as the sun peeked over the horizon.

J.D. had really taken charge. She had read on his resume that he had served in the Marines. He should have stayed in the service. At least if you got blown up, it was for your country, not for making out with your girlfriend.

The mall was warm and smelled of fresh cookies and coffee. The aroma beckoned and, rather than heading for her office, she pivoted in the direction of the Cookie Muncher. Rick raised an eyebrow when she ordered a snickerdoodle and a brownie, but wisely kept his mouth shut.

Henry and Margaret were sitting at a table outside the cookie shop. Laurie noticed that Henry was wearing a bright new jogging suit and equally bright walking shoes. She had priced an identical pair last week and almost fainted. She idly wondered where Henry had gotten the money. She had been under the impression that he was on a pretty strict income. She felt a flick of irritation as she realized the older man must have purchased the outfit to impress Margaret. Although Laurie had only met the woman a few weeks ago, she gave her the creeps. The way her black eyes watched every move Laurie made seemed odd. Surely she couldn't be jealous of the close relationship Henry and Laurie had developed? The man was old enough to be her grandfather for Pete's sake! Anyway, the whole mall knew that Henry was infatuated with the dark-haired beauty. Margaret wasn't an American, although she professed to be from the East coast. Laurie knew that with all the different ethnic backgrounds in and around New York that it was possible Margaret was from the Italian and Asian parents she claimed. Still, the faint accent Laurie picked up on wasn't New York or even vaguely Italian or Asian. Henry was captivated by the woman and Laurie didn't want to pry. She knew better than anyone—a person's background was no one's business.

Margaret was daintily sipping coffee and when she saw Laurie approach it turned to vinegar. Henry looked like a fool waving the girl over to the table like he did every morning. The man doted on her. It was disgusting.

"Let me tell you about the new play at the theater," Henry enthused, pulling out a chair for Laurie.

"Great." Laurie tried to be nice to Margaret for Henry's sake. "If Henry didn't keep me up on the local productions, I wouldn't have any idea what was going on. I can't ever get anyone to take me."

"Maybe that new security guard will."

"J.D.?"

"Henry tells me you two are an item." Margaret scooted her chair a little closer to Henry.

"No, not really. We had a date last night, but it was

a disaster. I don't think I'd better plan on seeing much of him."

"Oh, but you shouldn't give up." Margaret grabbed Laurie's hand. "You really should give it another try. You never know."

Henry patted the hand that covered Laurie's. "Now, Margaret, don't push her. This Westat character probably isn't right for her."

"But she really should give him a second chance." Margaret was adamant.

"Okay, Margaret, I promise to give it some thought." She didn't want to mention that J.D. would probably run screaming into the night at the very mention of her name.

"Laurie." Rick stepped out from behind the counter and waved at her. "Carrie called. She said there's a policeman waiting in your office." The tone of his voice said he would like an explanation.

"Thanks." Laurie gathered her discarded coat and purse. "Well, I better go finish making arrangements for Santa's arrival."

Henry seemed satisfied with her answer and she told her conscience that she hadn't really lied. She did have to finish the promo, but she knew the policeman was here for a much more sinister reason.

"Is everything okay?" Carrie whispered when Laurie walked in.

Laurie shrugged and picked up a stack of pink messages as she headed for her office.

"I guess you need me to answer more questions, Detective?" Tossing her coat onto the rack, she rounded her desk before facing the grim-faced detective.

"A few, if you don't mind." The detective sat down in the chair opposite her.

"I really don't know what else I can tell you. Obviously someone thinks I have something. Believe me, I wish I knew what."

"Are you sure you don't have any idea?"

Laurie could tell by the look on his face that he had already made up his mind as to her innocence. No matter what she said to the man, he wouldn't believe her. She fought the urge to shout obscenities. "I've told you that I don't."

"Maybe the federal boys can come up with something." Anderson watched her face as he informed her that federal agents had been called in.

"I hope so." Laurie began shifting papers on her desk, hoping the man could take a hint. "Is there anything else?"

"The fire chief said that wasn't just any homemade firecracker. Whoever put that baby together knew his stuff. If he had wanted it to go off your sister would be arranging your funeral today."

Laurie's spine tingled at the thought, but she refused to give Anderson the satisfaction of seeing that his crude words had upset her.

Seeing that she had no more to say the detective finally left. Laurie told Carrie to hold all calls.

Laurie slipped through the connecting door between her and Mr. Conway's office. She suspected her phone was tapped and prayed that James's was clear. Sitting in his large swivel chair she drummed her fingers on the oak desk. She felt awkward. Not only was the entire office exceedingly ostentatious, but since James was left-handed, everything was backward. She sat staring at the phone. Logically she realized the revulsion she was experiencing was perfectly normal. Once she picked up the phone and dialed that almost forgotten number, her life would be thrown back into the turmoil she had barely survived five years ago. Her head ached from the lack of sleep and the shock of the past several hours.

Reaching out with slightly trembling fingers, she punched out the numbers.

Four rings. "Please connect me with extension 447." She paused for a fortifying breath. "This is Laurie Morrison."

Another pause. Another shudder. Another voice.

"It's time to pay the piper."

"Now, Laurie . . ."

"Sorry, but you're not going to pacify me with a bunch of clap-trap." Her voice was steel-edged and steady.

"You were recently evaluated and received a high rating."

She hated the code words and hidden meanings. Why didn't they just say what they meant, her security had checked out.

"I don't care what rating I received at my last evaluation. As of today I am requesting another one. I would also like your opinion of the following people."

"Are you sure this is necessary?" The bored note in the man's voice didn't exactly inspire the confidence Laurie needed right now. "I want these people evaluated as soon as possible. Frankie Gonzales, Carrie Barstow, Pitsie Morrison, William Morrison, and Jon Derry Westat."

"That's quite a list."

"I want it done, and I hope you are able to do a more thorough job than the one you did the last time we worked together." Laurie didn't see the need for more conversation and hung up. She hated leaving the safety of her family and friends to someone else, but right now she didn't have the connections to be of much help.

J.D. slipped through the back door and just to be certain, he yelled for Pitsie and Laurie. Ascertaining the house was empty, he ventured in. He had spent two hours going through her office again. He had to have overlooked something. The trash bags they had taped over the broken window rattled with the wind and the house was a far cry from the warm, cheerful home it had been twenty-four hours ago.

Shifting into his "spy" mode, J.D. systematically began his search. He climbed the stairs to the attic and shuffled through years of family memorabilia. Working from one corner of a room to the next, he slowly made his way through the house. For six hours he poked and probed into every nook and cranny of Laurie's life. He had seen more nail polish, lipstick, panty hose, and feminine hygiene products than he had expected to see in a lifetime. He had found his breath quickening when he had searched through Laurie's underwear drawer. He had held tiny scraps of red and white lace that caused him to harden. The thought of peeling them off her delectable body took his mind completely off the task at hand. Purple silk teddies and white garter belts sent him from her room at break neck speed. Why didn't she wear those neon cotton things like Pitsie?

He had sifted through flour and sugar, searched for secret bank or code books, and even listened to their tapes for secret messages. He would have to find a way to get the tapes to the lab for more sophisticated tests.

He made his way down to the basement looking for a freezer filled with thousands of dollars disguised as a Sunday pot roast. His hands were frozen and he was covered with dirt, but it finally paid off. Down in a corner of the basement, carefully hidden behind a loose cinderblock, he hit paydirt. A stack of letters tied in a scarlet ribbon. He read the letters, choking on each term of endearment, each promise made. There was no doubt now. Every letter was signed by the one man TAT had positively identified as a member of the terrorists. A man that promised "his darling" a life together despite the overwhelming odds. Slipping one letter into the back pocket of his jeans for evidence, he gently tied the ribbon into a perfect bow and slid them back into their hiding place. His sigh echoed the stillness of his soul. He had never felt more betrayed. Not only had Laurie turned out to be his sworn enemy, but his own instincts had failed him. More than once his hunches had saved his skin, now he couldn't even trust himself. He'd finish this job for Clifton and then go so far underground no one but God could find him.

The sound of a truck pulling into the driveway brought him from his reverie and he flew up the basement steps to the back door. Slipping through the splintered wood, he quickly made his way to the alley. He had parked his car a couple of blocks away and by the time he slid behind the wheel, his cheeks were numb with the cold.

Passing down Laurie's street, he noticed a panel van parked in the driveway. Laurie must have gotten permission to have the glass replaced.

J.D. let his anger take over as he drove toward the mall. At least that was an emotion he was equipped to deal with.

Frankie and Laurie were in the storeroom and J.D. lounged against the door frame, watching Laurie struggle with a large crate. She was laughing at some remark of Frankie's when she caught sight of him. Was Frankie in cahoots with her? Did he know that the woman he admired and protected was an international killer? What would happen to the poor guy if he accidentally stumbled across her little secret?

Laurie's laughter hung in her throat at the sight of him. He looked like he wanted to kill someone. "Hi, there."

J.D. raised his hand to Frankie and casually strolled over to Laurie. "Looks like a job for a real man."

"Oh?" Laurie tested a grin. "Know where I might find one?"

"Cute, real cute." He easily lifted the crate and followed Laurie to the furthest corner of the room.

"Just put it there." Laurie really had no idea where she wanted the crate, she just wanted out of Frankie's listening range.

J.D. straightened to look into the eyes that had drawn more from him than any woman had ever done.

"I feel like I ought to apologize for last night."

"Why? Did you order a bomb tossed through your window?"

Though the remark was made in jest, Laurie flinched at the underlying harshness in his voice. "J.D., stop it. You could have been hurt or killed if that darn thing had been real." Laurie stopped and shook her head. "This is too incredible. I couldn't handle it if you got hurt."

J.D. grinned at her words. "Yeah, we wouldn't want anyone to get hurt, would we?"

"Well, I am sorry. About everything."

"Don't worry about it. I gotta tell you, though, that was the most interesting 'no' I've had in a long time." His eyes burned into hers, daring her.

Suddenly, like a break in the clouds, Laurie knew. He wasn't mad about the bomb, he was mad because she had turned him down! Of all the conceited, egotistical, macho cretins!

"Well, that's me, never a dull moment," she quipped, not bothering to disguise her anger.

J.D. recognized the anger for what it was, fear and pain. He knew she was calculating her next move. She had to be very careful how she handled her reaction to his attack. She couldn't afford to get too carried away or she might reveal some vital piece of information in her anger.

He had let himself get carried away last night and it could have been fatal. When he had reported to Clifton, he had felt like some untrained rookie on a training assignment.

"Westat, what better way to throw suspicion off of herself? Come on, man! That ticker was put together to do just exactly what it did. It was made out of materials that half the free world can buy at the corner hardware store. The only difference is the professional touch. Not enough to trace, but good enough to make sure they get the credit."

J.D. had murmured a few choice words and agreed. Still his gut wouldn't buy it. None of it. Even after finding those letters.

Laurie's green eyes glittered with fury. He knew he should keep his mouth shut, but if he got her mad enough, maybe she would let something slip. It was a tactic he had used quite successfully before.

"Yeah, it just didn't get quite as exciting as you and that dress advertised." He knew it was a hell of a thing to say.

"What's that supposed to mean?" Her fingers itched to slap that superior look off his face.

J.D. leaned down into her face. "Aw, come on, babe. All night long you were wiggling all over me. That dress was designed for seduction. I spent half the night wondering if you had any panties on. Do you have any idea what that does to a man?" J.D. snorted. "Of course you do. That was the whole idea, right, babe? You're one of those women who gets a thrill from teasing a man to the point of no return and then backs off." He felt like a class A bastard, but he had to push her. "All this junk about women being dominated by men. You probably think you're getting revenge for all the years of oppression. Well, one of these days some man won't know the rules." He grabbed her by the shoulder and twirled her around. He had to watch her. Had to make her lash out. "You're a real bi . . ."

Laurie struggled against him, twisting her head to keep him from seeing the tears streaming down her face. The accusations he had flung at her pierced her heart like daggers. "Stop it! Leave me alone."

"What the hell?" A woman's tears had never bothered him before. He knew they were merely tools of the trade and he had caused any number of women to cry and walked away without the tiniest pang of regret. Somehow knowing he was responsible for Laurie's tears, real or pretend, made him nauseated. Only moments before she had been angry, ready to hurl his insults back in his face. Now her shoulders slumped in defeat.

"I'm sorry, I didn't mean to hurt you, J.D." Her voice was barely more than a harsh whisper, but it roared in his ears.

"Hurt me?" He took her face in his hands and brought her eyes to meet his.

"I know women are supposed to be more liberated as far as these things go, but I want, no, I need, it to be special. I did want you to make love with me last night, or I would never have let things go so far." She brushed a coppery curl out of her eyes. "I'm really very careful about not leading men on. You may not believe that, but I just can't seem to think straight when I'm around you."

"Aw hell." J.D. wrapped her tightly in his arms, her head nestled against his chest. "I don't think you're a tease. You ought to be wringing my neck, not apologizing." He tangled his fingers in her hair. "I'm angry, tired, and more than a little frustrated, but I sure as hell shouldn't take it out on you."

Laurie grinned up at him. "Isn't it because of me that you are angry, tired, and frustrated?"

"Yeah, but I want you to know something. If you ask, I'll always stop."

"That's very sweet."

"What can I say, I'm a very sweet guy." The familiar cockiness was back in his grin. It had completely slipped his mind that he was holding his number one suspect in his arms. *Again!*

"Okay, sweet guy, I have two things to say to you." Laurie forced herself away from him.

"Shoot."

"One, if you ever speak to me like that again, I'll knock you forty ways from Sunday. You are not the only one who has worked up a little healthy frustration, you know."

"Yes, ma'am."

"And two, while I appreciate that you are willing to stop," she stepped back into the circle of his arms, "don't let me go too far."

"Too far?"

"I don't want you to be uncomfortable."

J.D. shot her a grin that said she didn't have anything to worry about. His lips caressed the top of her head and she found herself lamenting her height again.

"Excuse me."

J.D. and Laurie broke apart. Carrie had entered the back door and stood in the doorway, her face a lovely shade of red.

"Oh, Carrie! I, uh, that is . . . we were just . . ." With a helpless little shrug Laurie gave up.

J.D. winked at her. "She always seems to have trouble with her vocabulary when I'm fixin' to kiss her."

"Shut up." Her threat was idle.

"Do you want to argue or do you want to put Carrie out of her misery?"

"I just got back from lunch, but the answering service said Pitsie called a few minutes ago and said it was an emergency." She handed Laurie a stack of pink messages.

"Probably out of chocolate chip cookies," Laurie said, crossing to the phone on the back wall.

Her eyes narrowed as she realized the number on the slip was her next door neighbor's. Her pink tipped nails punched the numbers. "Hiya, kiddo."

With Pitsie's first words Laurie's entire body changed. Her hand clenched the receiver and her eyes glinted. J.D. noticed a flush creeping up her neck and the rapid pace of her breathing. "Stay there. Do not go back to the house. Don't even go outside. I don't have time to argue. Just do what I said and I'll be right there."

"What's wrong?" J.D.'s words broke into her frantically calculating thoughts.

"The house has been trashed. I've got to go."

"What are we standing around for?" He grabbed her elbow and propelled her toward the door.

"Should I call the police?" Carrie called after them.

"Yes." J.D. answered, never breaking stride.

SIX

J.D. had barely swung into the driveway when Laurie flung open the car door and shot toward the tiny white and red house next door. Pitsie flew out of the house and almost knocked Laurie to the ground. "It's awful. Everything is torn up, just like on T.V."

"I thought you were staying with Tiffanie?"

"She's coming back to get me. I wanted to get a few things for . . . but I don't have anything left!" The thought of her clothes shredded and flung across her room brought on a fresh onslaught of tears.

"It's okay, honey, I'll take care of everything." Laurie dug around in her purse. "You have Tiffanie take you to the mall and you can get a few new outfits."

"Really?" Pitsie's tears stopped and she stared in wonder at the plastic card in her hand.

"Really! Just remember I do have a limit on that thing."

"I'll be careful." Pitsie vowed. "I really needed some new stuff anyway. Most of that junk was so old I was mortified."

J.D. stared at Pitsie, his mouth open. One minute she had been crushed at the loss of her clothes and the next she resembled Wilma Flintstone shouting, "Charge it!" Were all teenagers this shallow?

Another thought flashed in his mind. Did Laurie solve all of Pitsie's problems with money? If so, she had to be making more than the government knew about.

He watched Laurie gently assure the elderly Mrs. Samuels that she didn't need a place to stay and coax the woman back out of the cold. No sooner was that accomplished than a pretty brunette in a bright red Suburban slid into the driveway behind his Bronco with only millimeters to spare.

"Hiya, Laurie, what are you doin' home? Is that spectacular lookin' guy with you? I couldn't believe it when Pitsie said somebody tried to blow up your house. I mean that is too weird. Ya know what I mean?" Tiffanie kept up her rapid-fire conversation, never noticing that no one bothered to answer her.

Laurie tucked them into the huge vehicle and waved them away. "That," she said smiling across the lawn at him, "was Hurricane Tiffanie."

"I'm exhausted." He led her toward the house, wondering again at a woman who could, having been informed her home had been ransacked, blithely hand her sister a charge card and send her to the mall. Damn, could she be so cold-hearted?

Laurie didn't hesitate on the threshold but squared her shoulders and barged right in. She had been terrified of falling apart in front of Pitsie. She had played down the entire episode as best she could. She had seen the confusion in both J.D. and Pitsie's eyes when she fished her charge card out for Pitsie. It wasn't usually the way she handled a crisis, but Pitsie had decided that if Laurie felt she could go shopping by herself, then there wasn't any real danger. Laurie had told Pitsie to go to the mall for the merchant's discount. The real reason was that she knew Pitsie would be safe there. With all those eyes watching Pitsie, whoever had started this little game wouldn't risk an attack on the girl.

The back door had been kicked the rest of the way off its hinges and the remnants of the kitchen table lay across the doorway. The floor was littered with the contents of the refrigerator and the cabinets. All through the house they encountered deliberate destruction. To the best of her ability she determined that nothing had been taken, only destroyed. This fact alone told her that it wasn't just vandals who had picked her home at random. Someone had done this to her for a specific reason. The question was who, or more importantly—*why?*

J.D. watched Laurie carefully pick her way through the remains of her life. The only flicker of emotion he had witnessed had been anger and confusion. Both normal emotions. But why no reaction? Why didn't she scream, or cry, or throw something? Even a real good cuss word would have been a relief from this unemotional inventory.

"I'd better call the police." Laurie steeled herself before looking at J.D. If she wasn't careful, she would fall apart and there was too much to be done.

J.D. nodded and watched her disappear into the bedroom. Had she forgotten Carrie was going to call them? He could hear her talking with someone. He absently poked at a torn cushion with the toe of his boot as he sidled closer to the door.

"No, I have no idea who could be responsible. That's why I called you."

J.D. could barely hear her now.

"No! Listen, I told you this morning, I am out of it!"

J.D. could tell Laurie wanted to scream the harshly whispered words. Who was she talking to? Out of what?

"Look, you owe me. I didn't want to resort to this type of tactic, but I will and you know I'm damn good at it."

J.D.'s eyebrows shot up at her choice of words.

"I don't have to tell you what will happen if I come forward. It may have been a long time ago, but it would still blow your rear off the map."

J.D. dared another inch or so toward the door. It would be tricky if she opened the door and he was standing any closer.

"I want someone put on Pitsie at all times."

Another inch couldn't hurt.

"Fine, you do that. I still expect to be top priority. You owe me. Don't forget it. I haven't." The last held a thinly veiled threat uttered in a deadly whisper that actually sent chills down his spine. For the first time, he could imagine that voice issuing a death order. Quickly stepping away from the door, J.D. assumed what he hoped was a natural stance. Plastering just the right amount of concern and curiosity on his face, he waited for Laurie. And waited. And waited. Finally, relaxing his pose, he ventured back toward the door. "Laurie?"

The door to her bedroom was probably the only one still in working order and he hesitantly knocked. "Babe, you okay in there?"

What was she doing? Finally, throwing caution to the wind, something he seemed to be getting pretty good at lately, he thrust open the door.

Laurie sat on the edge of what was left of her bed staring at what was obviously two halves of the same book. The leather was worn and well-fingered, the pages yellow and well-read. Her mouth moved, but no sound issued forth. Tears streamed from sightless eyes and her already fair skin had taken on a gray tinge. Her shoulders trembled with her silent sobs.

J.D. glanced at the torn Bible in her hands. Had he

really wanted a reaction from her? This was scary, even for him. He thought he was prepared for anything, but this almost catatonic grief tore him up.

He felt an unfamiliar lump lodge in the base of his throat and his eyes couldn't seem to focus. If she was what Clifton claimed, what kind of a game was this? She should have fallen apart in his arms, or at the very least ranted and raved. He eased onto the mattress beside her, but she didn't seem to be aware of him. Her hands were like ice as he tried to pry the torn Bible from her fingers. A wild look came into her eyes and an anguished cry ripped from her throat as he tried to take the book.

"Okay. Okay, baby, you keep it." J.D. watched her for a minute, trying to decide what to do. He finally shrugged and wrapped his arms around her. He hadn't been good for much else lately, but he was getting to be an expert at holding her.

By the time the police arrived, she had stopped shaking but was totally unresponsive. J.D. answered their questions as best he could under the circumstances.

"Do you want me to radio for an ambulance?" a young officer had asked.

"No, I'll take care of her." He gave the officers his address and phone number and requested that they give the information to Detective Anderson. He was sure the detective would have a few questions of his own.

After a few attempts at shaking Laurie out of whatever shell she had locked herself into, he hauled her into his arms and carried her to the Bronco. She hadn't spoken a word or moved since he had found her and he couldn't imagine her faking this kind of reaction. Damn it, it didn't make any sense!

Unless someone other than TAT was onto her. What had she said? She was "out of it." But out of what?

Maybe she was backing out of her commitment with the terrorists and they couldn't afford any loose ends. Possibly some other terrorist faction had located her? No, the bomb had been a warning, he'd bet his favorite flannel shirt on it. If she was backing out of the organization, maybe they were trying to tell her that she had better keep her mouth shut. It made sense, marginally. He knew for certain that she couldn't be just an innocent bystander now. With a large leap of the imagination, he could believe the bomb had been a coincidence. It had happened before. Innocent folks had their homes invaded everyday. But did innocent people have bombs tossed through their windows *and* their homes ransacked within a twenty-four hour period? That was tough to swallow.

Calling himself a rather ugly name for renting an upstairs apartment, he eventually managed to get Laurie through his door and onto his couch. She sat there on top of several back issues of *Sports Illustrated* and one or two dirty socks. Housekeeping wasn't his forte. He didn't bring women to his place for several reasons and that was one of them. About once a month he tunneled through everything and cleaned. He had enough underwear and shirts to last two weeks so he only had to make the trek to the laundry room in the basement twice a month. He lived like a bachelor and he liked it that way. Nobody yelling at him to pick up his boots or underwear. No healthy balanced meals washed down with foamy glasses of milk. He'd had enough of that in the Marines. Chalk it up to a latent rebellious tendency.

Laurie didn't seem to notice. He had finally managed to pry the Bible from her, but her fingers were still slightly curved as if she held it. Only last night she had seemed so vibrant. Full of life and color. Now she seemed, he didn't know, faded.

"Oh." Laurie's eyes brightened with unshed tears. "They've found you."

J.D. eased himself down next to her. "Who found me, sweetheart?" His gut clenched with self-loathing. She needed care not an inquisition.

"Look what they did to your home." She automatically began straightening the magazines on the coffee table.

J.D. stilled her hands with his. "No one's been here."

"But . . . but look at this mess."

"Baby doll, I made this mess." He found himself almost apologizing for the way he chose to live his life. Hell, what was wrong with him? He liked the way he lived. For too many years he had been required to answer to every Tom, Dick, and Harry that outranked him. When he had left the Marines behind he had sworn never to answer to anyone for anything. "I like that 'lived in' look."

"Ironic, isn't it." She picked up his hand and began pushing the cuticle on his thumbnail. "The home I love has been turned into something you would feel comfortable in." Although she was talking, her voice was dull and empty.

"Aw, babe, that's like comparing swimming lessons to a shipwreck. You learn how to swim, but your choice is taken away." He leaned back against the couch, pulling her with him. "If I ever find the bastards that shipwrecked you, I'll kill 'em."

For once Laurie didn't correct his language. She looked at him and saw no humor in his eyes. He meant what he said. He was too caring a man to let anyone hurt a woman, any woman, and sit idly by. It scared her to think that this adorable man would risk his life for her. And it would be his life, she knew that. Just as she knew she would have to make very sure it never came to that. She knew what kind of people were out there waiting for her to slip up. If they ever found out that this precious man held her heart, he was a dead man.

"Babe?"

She realized J.D. had asked her something and she had no idea what. "Fine."

He seemed pleased with her answer and pulled her to her feet. He kept up a steady chatter of nonsense while they made their way to the Bronco. She smiled when J.D. reached over to check her seat belt. She still had no idea where they were headed and she was too embarrassed to ask.

"What are we doing here?" When they pulled into the parking lot at the mall, she had to ask.

"Well, I heard you tell Pitsie that the merchants give you a discount. I figured this would be where you wanted to go." He looked at her, a scowl pulled his eyebrows together. "You sure you feel up to shopping?"

"Shopping?"

"Babe, I think we'd better take you to see your doctor." He inserted his key back into the ignition.

"No, no. I just . . ." Come on, Laurie, think. "I didn't think you would want to go with me." Good girl, that made sense, all men hated to shop.

"Are you kiddin'? I love to shop." The gleam in his eye told her it was true. So much for that theory.

Laurie lifted her shoulders in a delicate shrug. "Let's go, but don't say I didn't warn you."

J.D. lifted her out of the Bronco and set her down. "Don't worry, I'm a big boy."

"You sure are." Laurie didn't realize she had spoken out loud until she heard his deep chuckle beside her.

Since it was after five, Carrie and Frankie had already gone home and the office was dark and quiet. She and J.D. left their coats in her office and she checked her messages.

"Somethin' wrong?"

Laurie glanced up at him. "No, nothing that won't wait."

J.D. took her hand and slid her keys from her grasp. "I'll put these in my pocket and you can leave your purse here."

"Normally I would, but with all these break-ins I think I'll feel better if I keep it with me. Besides, you can hold it for me while I try on clothes."

"That's what I was afraid of." He grimaced.

"Ha! I thought you said you *loved* shopping. Are you going to chicken out on me?" She wiggled her eyebrows.

"Chicken? Me? Bite your tongue." J.D. made a production of opening the door and bowing as she walked past him.

She led him to the western store situated next to the office. The one item of clothing she couldn't do without was a good pair of jeans. Gloria, the owner, was in the store that day and the way she rushed at Laurie told her that Pitsie had already been there.

"Good goshamighty, Laurie, I can't believe what Pitsie told me." Her platinum blonde hair had been teased and sculpted into a style reminiscent of Dolly Parton and she clanked with several impressive pieces of turquoise jewelry.

"I feel like I'm starring in the Sunday night movie." Laurie returned the tall woman's hug and had to extricate her hair from the large squash-blossom necklace around Gloria's neck.

"Hello, J.D. I'm glad to see you're providing a little extra security." She shook his hand firmly. "She's real special."

Neither Laurie nor J.D. missed the meaning hidden behind Gloria's words. The whole mall must be aware they were seeing each other and now J.D. was being put to the test. Most of the time Laurie loved being a part of the "mall family," but at times they could be as trying as a real one.

"I take it Pitsie has already been here. Don't tell me the damage, I don't think I could take it right now." Laurie shook her head and began thumbing through a rack of gorgeous suede skirts and tops. Boy, wouldn't she love to be able to afford one of them. Especially the deep purple. It was the plainest of the designs, a simple shirtwaist. The tiny bit of fringe adorning the yolk of the shirt and the bottom of the full skirt gave it just an added flair.

"Do you like that, babe?" J.D. reached up to finger the soft material she was holding.

"Who wouldn't! I'm afraid it's just a tad out of my price range though." Laurie hung the dress back on the rack with only a tiny sigh of regret and headed for the plain jeans Gloria stacked against the back wall. Gloria believed if she hid them in the back of the store, her customers would never find them and would purchase the more expensive ones attractively arranged in the front of the store. Too bad, Laurie thought. She had lived on a budget long enough to know where to find every bargain in town. Most of her friends would die if they ever found out that the majority of her jewelry and accessories were not purchased at some trendy boutique, but at the local weekend flea market. She wondered if it would be open on Friday, too, since this was Thanksgiving week. She had seen a great purse a few weeks ago.

"Laurie! You just get your fanny away from those tacky jeans right now."

"Uh oh," Laurie muttered under her breath. She hated the fact that she could only afford to buy from Gloria because of the discount and now Gloria would try and steer her toward the higher priced items.

"Now I know what's runnin' through your mind, honey. You don't have to worry about a thing. I already let Pitsie pick out a few things on the house and you are gonna do the same thing."

Laurie opened her mouth to protest and caught J.D.'s amused expression over Gloria's head. "No, Gloria . . ."

"Honey, you know I make an indecent living out of my stores and if I want to do this for you, I will." She shook an absurdly long fingernail in Laurie's face. "As a matter of fact, I've already put a few things back. And don't you dare try and spoil this for me." She rushed on without letting Laurie get a word in. "The good Lord just gave me ornery old boys and I never get to dress little girls. I just had a ball with Pitsie and now it's your turn."

"Yes, ma'am." Laurie couldn't help but grin at Gloria's excitement. She was already thinking of a way to repay Gloria's kindness, but for now she wouldn't hurt her feelings.

"Good. Now, I laid back that little suede number in blue, but I think the purple will be much better with your hair. And I think the matching boots will really set it off. I gave Pitsie a pair of the red ones and she promised she'd share." Gloria rattled on and on, offering advice on what needed a belt and what could use a scarf. By the time they left Laurie felt as if she had stumbled through the looking glass. It was only the beginning.

At every store the merchants refused to let her pay for a thing. By the time they stopped in front of the bed and bath store she was in tears.

"Oh, J.D., a few hours ago I was so scared and worried. I felt it was up to me to take care of everything. Now look at me. I'm not used to being so pampered." Her voice lowered a notch. "Not used to feeling so secure."

J.D. held her against him for a quick hug that was as much for him as it was for her. He had watched Laurie as they went from store to store. She was such a special woman that it galled him to realize that no one ever did anything for her. He prayed he was right to listen to his heart instead of his head.

"I'm gonna take these back to the office while you pick out your towels or whatever. Just wait for me before you go to that fancy underwear place."

Laurie brazenly swatted his retreating and very well shaped rear-end and silently vowed to save the "fancy underwear place" for another time.

Since she wasn't being allowed to pay for anything, she was extremely careful to select only a minimum in each store. While Gloria had several stores to keep her in the black, most of the owners really couldn't afford to give merchandise away.

The bed and bath store was one of Laurie's favorite places. She had often longed for the gorgeous bedroom ensembles so elegantly displayed. Yards of satin and lace piled with a mountain of fluffy pillows sounded like just the boost she needed. Maybe she would put one on lay-away.

"I've got just the thing." Mrs. Hannah, the owner, led her to the back of the store. "You know, I don't think our Merchant's Association has ever voted for anything unanimously, but when that fellow of yours called and asked if there wasn't something we could do for ya'll, there wasn't one member who wasn't willing to do everything they could."

Laurie turned to stare at the large woman. J.D.?

"My goodness, you're just like family. Everytime one of us is sick or needs something, there you are taking up a collection, sending flowers, and visiting. Matter of fact, you treat me better than some of my own flesh and blood."

"I'm not going to have any make-up left on." Laurie sniffled and Mrs. Hannah reached into the pocket of her dress and handed Laurie a fresh tissue. The motherly gesture made her tears flow even faster.

"Now quit that before I join you," Mrs. Hannah ordered and led Laurie to a display bed covered with the most fabulous spread Laurie had ever seen. It was a polished cotton material that gleamed. The background was a deep forest green with an abstract design of cream and navy splashed across it. It wasn't the ultra feminine satin and lace she had envisioned, but it was gorgeous. Heavy and plush, Laurie could picture J.D. sprawled naked across . . . Good grief, what was the matter with her? Imagine, standing in the middle of a store dreaming about naked men. Well, okay, so it was only one naked man, but hoo boy!

She blushed under Mrs. Hannah's knowing look. "I didn't figure you would be wanting anything too frilly. Most men are real uncomfortable around that sort of fluff. I can just picture your young man in this."

Laurie tried, but couldn't keep the astonished look off her face. "Oh, well . . ."

"Now don't looked so shocked. I do have eight children, you know. I'm well acquainted with how a man looks in bed. Believe you me, the colors and prints that you have in your boudoir can make all the difference." Her eyes took on a dreamy glow. "One time I redid my bedroom in pink flowers. That was why there are more years between my middle boys than any of the rest. Mr. Hannah just didn't feel like it was his bedroom, too."

"But it won't be in J.D.'s bedroom." Laurie felt like she had to put up some kind of protest.

Mrs. Hannah didn't pay any attention as she went on to explain that the entire ensemble had been on layaway for several months. The woman had never come back to finish paying for it.

"Well, I can only hold them for so long and then I put them back on the floor. I've already made my money back on it. I'm going to throw in a set of kitchen towels and a few other knick knacks that are cluttering up the storeroom. Most of it is stock that we just couldn't move so I'm not being all that generous."

Laurie agreed that the bedspread would be perfect if only she had a bed to put it on.

"Well, you'll be getting insurance money, won't you?"

"My gosh, I haven't even called my agent yet." Her mind was already swirling with the new information Mrs. Hannah had given her. J.D. was responsible for all of this. He sure was making it hard not to fall in love with him.

"Hi, there, did you pick out something pink and lacy?" J.D. was leaning against the wall outside the store sipping a soft drink.

"No, it's not pink or lacy." Laurie reached up and took the drink from him. "As a matter of fact, Mrs. Hannah already had one picked out for us."

"Us?" Was that his voice that squeaked?

"Um hum, she said that it would make you more comfortable in my boudoir." Laurie relished watching the faint pink blush that crept up his neck.

"Comfortable?" There was that damned squeak again.

"Yeah. Said she could just picture you in my bed."

"What is she, some kind of dirty old lady?"

"Not hardly. She just thinks our relationship is much farther along than it actually is. I didn't want her to be disillusioned." Laurie sucked down the last of his drink before handing the empty cup back to him.

"Gee thanks." He lofted the cup through the air and into one of the trash receptacles in the mall.

"Anytime." The fantasy of J.D. in her bed had somehow made her feel closer to him. She enjoyed the way they easily teased each other. There was an intimacy about it that she had never experienced before.

"Are we headed for The Bewitching Hour?"

"I believe I can pick out my own underthings, thank you." Laurie tried to sound stern, but didn't quite carry it off. "Besides, the Bewitching Hour doesn't exactly carry your basic everyday underwear."

J.D. opened his mouth to say that her underwear was far from basic. Then he remembered that she knew nothing of his excursion through her panties that morning. "Aw, come on. It can't hurt to look."

Laurie found herself reluctantly hauled to the store. She stood there reluctantly amid the masses of red lace and black satin dreading the next few minutes.

"Hi, Laurie, we just got in some great new stuff. It's too bad about what happened."

"Thanks, Monica. I really just need a few basics to tide me over until the insurance comes in."

"You?" Monica shouted. "You want something basic?"

"Yes," Laurie growled, hoping the woman would get the hint.

"But, Laurie, you never buy anything basic. Lord, if I had your figure I wouldn't either." Monica never took her eyes off J.D. "I've got another one of those purple teddies around here somewhere."

"I'll just browse," said J.D.

"Yeah, you do that, J.D., you just do that." Laurie glared at him. She hadn't exactly lied. A purple silk teddie was basic, for her.

She'd never felt comfortable in the basic working woman's wardrobe, so exquisite lingerie helped make her feel better. James Conway was a stickler for "power" dressing. She and Carrie were required to wear staid grey and navy suits with only the occasional scarf to relieve the severity. She used his frequent absences to dress with her usual flair. It would be hard to return to the dress code when he returned. She didn't think she could make it through the day without her silk underwear shielding her.

"I called the boss man and he said you were covered up to two hundred," Monica informed her, pulling several bra and panty sets onto the counter for her approval.

"Great." Laurie selected several sets in a wide range of colors. She tried not to notice J.D. flicking through the high priced negligees. He pulled a few out for inspection.

"What about something like this?" He held up a frothy baby blue monstrosity.

"Oh, that's pretty, but I don't usually wear . . ." Laurie stopped cold as she realized what she was saying. What she wore to bed was none of his business. The fact that she usually wore old worn out T-shirts usually didn't embarrass her. They were comfortable, practical, and who needed pretty sleepwear when you climbed into bed alone every night? J.D. didn't need to know that either.

"Wear what?" J.D.'s voice had taken on a huskiness that told her he had finished her sentence in his mind. From the look on his face she realized he thought she slept in the nude. Too embarrassed to correct his erroneous conclusion, she turned back to Monica for the gaily colored shopping bag containing her selections.

Monica waved them off with a reminder that she was expecting a new shipment of French lingerie next week.

"What's so special about French underwear?"

"Nothing! J.D., can we please find something else besides my underwear to discuss?"

"We could discuss what you sleep in," he offered.

"Fine. Only you go first." There, put him on the defensive.

"Sure. I sleep in my underwear. Plain old Fruit of the Looms." He placed his hand on the small of her back and steered her through the crowd. "I tried sleeping in the buff once, but I was afraid I might roll onto something important." This he said with a perfectly straight face.

"Dream on."

"When ya got it, flaunt it."

Laurie led him into the last shop on her list. "Save me from egotistical men, Mary."

Mary Stephens looked every inch the cosmetologist in her pink overcoat and perfectly made-up face. "Laurie, I knew you would be in so I've already pulled your card."

"I don't think you need me for this, so I'll just wander around." J.D. backed out of the door of the heavily perfumed shop.

"I do carry cosmetics for men," Mary offered but J.D. just kept on walking. He'd seen a little number back in The Bewitching Hour that Laurie needed. Actually, it was something he had pictured her in so exquisitely, he needed it. He could only hope that the time would come when he could see it on her. He wondered if they allowed overnight visitors in prison. His gut still told him it would never happen, but his mind argued otherwise. Even if she wanted out badly enough to help the government, she would still have to serve some time. Especially if she had been as close to the top as Clifton suspected.

"Well, hello again." J.D. noticed Monica's voice had dropped a full octave in her clumsy attempt to be sexy. "Was there anything else I could do for you?"

"I wondered if you have that little black number in Laurie's size." He indicated a black silk baby doll that was basically held together with purple ribbons and a lot of luck.

"But Laurie never buys nightwear. I believe she told me she wears an old T-shirt." Monica wrinkled her nose and lowered her eyelashes. "I've never understood why any woman would want to do something like that.

I personally enjoy pretty evening clothes." She held the nightgown up against her. "I'd be more than happy to model anything in the store for you."

"Well, that's real nice." J.D. paused for effect. "Maybe I'll bring Laurie back and you can model some of this stuff for us and let her decide what she would like best." There, deal with that, you catty little witch.

"I'm sure you know what you want. Will this be cash or charge?" Her voice had returned to its normal octave and she didn't even bother to wiggle as she walked to the cash register.

J.D. made the purchase and even had Monica wrap the nightie in a beautiful package. If it was a present, Laurie couldn't turn it down. Could she?

Laurie had only spent a few minutes with Mary and had been looking for J.D. when she spotted him in The Bewitching Hour. She knew Monica was divorced and looking, but she hadn't really considered that J.D. might be interested. Laurie approached the door cautiously and when she heard Monica offer to model a slinky black bit of silk her blood boiled. Who did the woman think she was? J.D. was hers. She was about to charge into the store and stake her claim when she heard J.D. say that he thought it would be nice. Nice! She had whirled around mid-step before listening to any more. Her face flushed with humiliation. Of course J.D. would be interested in Monica. She was a fairly attractive woman who let it be known that she enjoyed life to the fullest. Laurie had often felt sympathy for the woman. Sympathy! Shoot, Monica probably knew exactly how to make a man feel comfortable in her bedroom without benefit of a properly colored bedspread.

Monica probably felt sorry for poor little Laurie. All that fancy underwear and nowhere to go. Besides, Laurie realized, she had no hold on J.D. He would enjoy an evening with a woman not facing a catastrophe every few minutes. He had only done all this for her because he was a nice guy. He had only called all the merchants for help because he wanted her out of his hair. Sure, the sooner she replaced her belongings the sooner she would be out of his way! She had been so blinded by her irrational fantasies of someone to lean on that she had read more into his kindness than he intended. Well, it was time she remembered who she was, and what she was capable of. She didn't need a man. She might want him, but she didn't need him. She would thank him kindly and then have him drive her to a hotel.

Her car! It was still in the parking lot. She had forgotten that J.D. drove her to the house after Pitsie's call. Of course he had her keys, but luckily she had an extra set in her desk and she knew where Frankie hid the extra key to the office. Deciding to put off any confrontations with J.D. until she was in a much better frame of mind, she flew to the office and grabbed her packages. Slipping through the back storeroom, she headed for her car. She sent up a prayer of thanks that the snow had stopped long enough for the snowplows to clear the road, and she headed across the Interstate to one of the hotels.

Monica could give J.D. a full fashion show for all she cared. She was a grown woman. Entirely self-supporting. The very idea that a man should take care of her was ludicrous. She absolutely did not need him! Oh yeah, Bozo! Then why are you crying so hard you can't see straight?

SEVEN

J.D. had circled the mall for the third time with no sign of Laurie. Where the heck was she? He had learned from Mary that she had left the make-up shop after only a few minutes and no one else had seen her. The small flutter in the pit of his stomach had to be indigestion. He was a trained professional. Professionals did not panic! Professionals did not break out in a cold sweat just because their girlfriend was lost in a shopping mall. Even when their girlfriend was a suspected felon. He was walking fast because he needed the exercise. Finally, he thought of the office. "Some professional you are."

He reined in his desire to sprint across the mall to the office suite. He knew she had to be there. But she wasn't.

The office was locked up tighter than a drum and he had her set of keys so she couldn't get in. He unlocked the door and decided to wait for her to show up. He had barely stepped in the office when it hit him. The packages were gone. Every bundle and bag he had tossed inside the door was gone. He double checked. Yep, he still had the keys and the sacks were gone. Whistling the music from the *Twilight Zone*, he stepped inside Laurie's office. Her coat was gone but his was lying on the floor. He quickly scanned the room and noticed her desk drawer was half open. He approached the desk cautiously, praying he didn't find a ransom note or a chopped off little finger with shiny pink nail polish. No, nothing wrong. But someone had been in her desk. Someone who might very well be hurting her right now. He had to find her.

Quickly locking the outer office door, he headed for his car. Mentally calculating what the best course of action was he forced himself to sit calmly for a minute. He leaned back in his seat and breathed in the faint smell of Laurie's perfume that lingered in the Bronco. He closed his eyes and visualized the last few hours. Something was wrong. What was it? The answer teased him from somewhere inside the jumbled mass of his brain. He visualized the wreckage of Laurie's home, the shops and their owners. Laurie, catatonic and animated. There was something out of place. One tiny scene that didn't quite fit. Suddenly, he glanced down at the parking space where her car should be. Gone! Hell, she hadn't been kidnapped, she had just left. Left him sitting there with a palpitating heart and sweaty palms. Great, just great. You've really gone over the deep end, old boy. Plumb lost it for a redhead who wears purple underwear. It was plain that Ms. Laurie Morrison could take care of herself. She certainly didn't need him. He ought to go back and take Monica up on her offer. He knew that wasn't the answer. Pretty as Monica was, she hadn't stirred even one stray hormone. She had all but laid down on the floor right there and he had felt sorry for her. He could tell himself that he was a forward thinking guy and deeply concerned about sexually transmitted diseases. He could tell himself that, but he knew it wasn't entirely true. If Laurie had offered herself, he would have been on her like flies on honey. The simple fact was: he wanted Laurie. Anytime, anywhere, anyhow, and he would be damned if she was just going to go off and leave him without any explanation at all. He had been a real prince today and she owed him that much. It was a pretty safe bet that she had gone to a hotel and it shouldn't be too hard to determine which one.

A few minutes later he spotted her car at the hotel directly across the Interstate. At least she wasn't trying to hide from him.

He easily obtained her room number from the pretty blonde at the front desk. Amazing what a man carrying a present and a handful of flowers could get away with. Not even stopping to think about what he was doing, he stalked to her room and beat on the door.

"Who is it?"

"Complimentary coffee and newspaper, ma'am." J.D. stood well away from the door so she couldn't see him through the peephole.

"I didn't order anything."

"It's compliments of the hotel, ma'am." J.D.'s voice strained as he strived to disguise it.

"Oh, okay." She didn't usually drink coffee, especially at eight o'clock at night, but at least it would give her something to do until she received her phone call.

She had barely turned the doorknob when the door was being forcefully thrust open. Old survival instincts sprang to life, and she sent a crippling kick to the intruder's lower mid-section followed by a set of quick jabs to the head and neck. The man crumbled at her feet with a sharp cry of pain. Her breath came in quick puffs after the unexpected exercise and her body flushed with the adrenalin surging through it.

Assuming an offensive stance, she surveyed her victim. Good grief, she had just K.O.'d the man of her dreams. He was lying in a fetal tuck making the most agonizing noise. A package wrapped in pink foil paper was crushed beneath him and half a dozen peach hued roses were scattered on the floor. He had stopped making that strangled noise and was lying perfectly still. She closed the door and bent over him.

"J.D.?" Great, he was out like a light. "J.D., honey?"

His breathing was so shallow she could barely detect the rise and fall of his chest. His face had relaxed and if she hadn't known better, she would have thought him asleep. She reached out with trembling fingers to caress his cheek. The rough stubble of his five o'clock shadow rasped her palm.

J.D.'s hand shot up and grabbed her wrist, effectively throwing her off-balance from her squatted position.

"What . . .!" Laurie shrieked as J.D. quickly rolled on top of her.

"Not exactly the greeting I had in mind, darlin'." He let his full weight rest on her briefly before rising up on his elbows, his long legs nestled between her much shorter ones. "Not exactly the way I pictured us in this position either."

"Get off!" He held her wrists in one large hand above her head, so she could only buck against him.

"Here now, darlin'. Much more of that bumpin' and grindin' and I won't be held responsible." He ground his pelvis against her for emphasis.

"You are sick!" she spat out, but held still all the same.

"Could be. I'll let you up in a minute. As soon as I'm sure you won't condemn me to a childless-life." His mouth hovered inches from hers. "Now you just lie there like a good little girl until I'm through."

"I will not."

"Laurie darlin', if you don't keep those delectable lips shut, I'll just have to take you up on your offer.

You decide, do we talk, or do we . . . ?" He let the innuendo hang.

"Talk."

"Fine. Now the first thing I expect from you will be an apology." He ignored the look of outrage that crossed her face. "That was pretty low, leaving me at the mall." He placed a gentle kiss on her nose. She snorted. "Don't worry, I'll forgive you."

Laurie humphed as best she could and turned her eyes from that penetrating blue gaze.

"Aw now, don't be like that. Hell, I've been a prince of a guy today. I let you say bad things about my home. I trotted along after you through the mall like a faithful hound dog lugging bag and baggage." He trailed hot, moist kisses on the delicate hollow of her exposed neck.

Deciding she couldn't handle that particular brand of torture and retain her anger, she faced him. J.D. knew she was fighting to stay angry, but he also saw the hot desire in her eyes. He wondered if she was even aware of how turned on she was. Of how her thighs were pressing against his. "I even had to face down that Monica to buy you a present."

Laurie's eyes flashed and her lips opened slightly. It was all the encouragement he needed. He took her mouth in a kiss so hot, he wondered if they would set off the sprinkler system. Laurie launched herself into the kiss with full abandon. Her tongue traced the inner flesh of his lower lip, drawing him in. He nibbled and suckled on her lips until they were both moaning with the need for each other. He longed to release her hands and feel them on his skin but he was still afraid this was a set-up. He had to stop now, before he was too mindless with wanting her to stay on top of the situation.

Her eyes were feverish as she glanced up at him. "Why did you stop?" She looked like a little girl who had just lost her all-day sucker.

"I think we have a few things to clear up."

"Oh." One kiss and the last twenty-four hours had completely slipped her mind. "I'm sorry I left you, but I thought you were interested in Monica."

"The man-eater?" His eyebrows shot up and he relaxed his hold on her.

"I heard her offer to model for you and you did say it would be nice." Better not forget all your pride, Laurie.

"I don't suppose you've ever heard that eavesdroppers never hear anything nice?"

"I was not eavesdropping!"

"Okay, okay calm down. But if you had 'not eavesdropped' for a few more seconds you would have heard me suggest that she could model for both of us."

"Oh."

"You better quit saying that," he warned.

"What?"

"When you say 'oh' like that it makes you look like you're ready to be kissed."

"Oh." A dimple played in Laurie's left cheek.

"Yeah, now stop it or we'll never finish this discussion."

"Oh?"

"You little witch." Everything else was forgotten in another mind-blowing kiss. She clung to him as they rolled across the thick carpet. Their legs tangled and Laurie felt a familiar heaviness. She was aware of the heat and the incredible throbbing of her heart.

"Babe, we gotta stop." His voice barely penetrated the fog of her desire.

"No." Was that pitiful plea hers?

"Darlin', we both know that in a matter of minutes I'm gonna be inside you right here on the floor."

The very thought sent shockwaves through her and she ground against him automatically, not realizing the stress she was adding to the situation.

"Don't!" He held her tight against him so she couldn't

move. "If you keep that up, I won't be able to stop and I have to."

Laurie whimpered against his neck.

"Look at me." He forced her eyes to his. "This is my point of no return. I didn't think I had one, but this is it." He could feel her mentally pull away from him, even though she was plastered against his length. "Precious, you told me you need it to be special. Believe me, it is gonna be fantastic no matter where or how, but if I take you now, half-dressed on the floor of some hotel room . . . Hell, that's about as special as the back seat of a Volkswagen."

He felt her embarrassment die. "Laurie, when we make love, I want it to be so special that you'll never have cause to regret it." He reached up and gently brushed her tangled hair out of her face. She was looking at him with such love in her eyes, that it made him want to strut like a teenager after his first time. It had been a long time since anyone had made him feel that way.

Laurie took a few minutes to regain her composure. She had only played this scene with a clear objective before and was at a loss. What did she do now? Thank him for his clear head and sensitivity? She didn't protest as he helped her up.

"Where did you learn to move like that?" he asked, reaching up to rub the back of his neck.

"In the back seat of a Volkswagen." She couldn't help teasing him.

"Not that, you ninny." He grabbed her hand and tugged her to him. "I meant the G.I. Joe moves."

"I know." She replaced his hand and massaged his shoulders. "Bubba taught me. When he went into the service he insisted that Pitsie and I know how to take care of ourselves."

"Must be some teacher." He bent down and picked up the crushed pink box. "This is for you."

"Thank you."

"If you don't like it you can exchange it." He indicated the package.

Laurie sat down on the edge of the bed and tore off what was left of the paper. "J.D., you shouldn't be buying me things like this."

"Why not?" He eased down next to her. Even sitting fully clothed on a bed with her aroused him. This was ridiculous.

"A man does not buy a nightie like this for a woman he hasn't even known a week." Her face flamed as she looked at the tiny scraps of black silk.

"That's a bunch of crud." J.D. took the nightie from her and stuffed it back into the box. The dad-burned thing hadn't looked near that sexy when Monica had held it up. "Shoot, my grandparents only knew each other for two weeks before they got married."

"Two weeks! Now I know where your hot blood comes from." She tried to pull the nightie from the box but he took it away.

"Yep. Granny said she knew all she needed to know." A huge grin spread across his face. "She said Grandpa was an honest, hard-working, Christian man that curled her toes by just looking at her."

"Did their marriage work?"

"You bet. I've never seen any two people more devoted to each other. Right up until the day my grandpa died he worshipped her."

"He died first?" She could see the tears sneak into J.D.'s eyes and fell more in love with him.

"He died when I was about twenty. Granny died a couple of years ago. She caught the flu and by the time I could make my way back here and force her to go to the hospital, it was too late." He cleared his throat. "The last breath she took held my grandpa's name."

Laurie let her tears slide unchecked. No wonder this man was so caring and sensitive. Even if he didn't know it. Anyone who came from such wonderful people had to be special. "I don't think love like that exists anymore."

"You never know." His eyes held hers for a heartbeat. He noticed the dark circles under her eyes and decided she was too exhausted physically and mentally to carry this conversation any further. "I think it's time you got to bed. Your eyes look like two burnt holes in a blanket."

"Was that something Granny used to say?"

"Yeah, she was full of old sayings and platitudes. My grandpa always answered everything with scripture."

Laurie began heading for the bathroom and a tubful of bubbles. "My mom was the same way."

"Yet another thing we have in common." J.D. picked up the room-service menu and didn't hear her reply.

As soon as he heard the water running, he quickly called the front desk and booked the adjoining room. Luckily it was empty and he didn't have to pull any strings. He quietly unlocked the connecting door. He realized it was probably better if Laurie didn't know he was babysitting. Clifton had informed him that two agents would be taking his place at the mall tonight. Clifton seemed to think J.D. was overlooking something. J.D. was glad he could stick close to Laurie. He hadn't told Clifton yet but he was positive Laurie was being set up by someone. There were too many loose ends. For one thing, if Laurie was so hot for this "letter writer," why could he set her on fire with the simplest touch? Where was all the money?

"J.D.?" Laurie peeked her head out of the bathroom and a puff of steam escaped.

"Whatcha need, babe?" It was all he could do not to fling the door open to see if the rest of her was as flushed as her face.

"I don't have anything to wear. I didn't buy any pajamas."

J.D. couldn't resist glancing at the enormous pile of boxes and sacks in the corner. "Nothing?"

"I didn't exactly plan on company," she said pointedly.

J.D. shook his head in wonderment of the female species, and began unbuttoning his flannel shirt. "Here take this."

"What will you wear? You can't exactly strut through the lobby like that." She took the offered shirt nonetheless. She tried not to stare at J.D.'s half-naked body. Clothed he was imposing, but like this he was amazing. How did he maintain his tan in the middle of November?

J.D. caught her stare and was oddly embarrassed. He was normally the one doing the staring and he wasn't sure how to respond to the admiration in her eyes. "If I zip up my coat, no one will be the wiser."

Laurie quickly slid into the warm flannel that smelled so strongly of J.D. Great, she'd have to smell him all night.

"I ordered some soup and sandwiches, they should be here by now." J.D. hardly knew what he was saying. There ought to be a law against looking that good in a flannel shirt that was ten times too big. No wonder she didn't wear sexy nightgowns, they would be redundant. Although her legs weren't long, they were perfectly shaped. In fact, her whole body looked like someone had stuck Marilyn Monroe in the dryer and shrunk her.

"I really think I'm too tired to eat." Laurie yawned as if to prove her point.

"You better try anyway. Besides I ordered for two

and I hate eating alone." He pulled back the bedspread and helped her into bed.

"Okay, I'll stay up until you eat." She tugged the covers up over her breasts and tucked them under her arms. She was too aware of the sexual tension between them to take any more chances.

J.D. was equally aware that it wouldn't take much to set them off. Luckily the dinner arrived before he made a total fool of himself and jumped into bed with her.

She had been right about being too tired. J.D. looked up to admonish her about not eating and noticed that her head had fallen back against the pillows and her breathing was soft and regular. J.D. finished his supper and then polished off hers. After making sure her door was secure, he slipped into his room. He was expecting a call from Clifton. There was more than one question he wanted an answer for.

The smell of hot cinnamon forced its way into her sleeping brain and Laurie slowly opened her eyes. J.D. was bustling around the table, laying out plastic silverware and Styrofoam cups. He had on a bright blue T-shirt that proudly bore the name of the hotel across the front.

"Mornin', glory." He smiled when he noticed her.

"What are you doing here?" She pushed herself up in the bed and shuddered to think what she must look like. She had slept hard during the night and from the looks of the bed she had done a fair share of tossing and turning.

"One ice-cold Dr. Pepper and two steaming, fresh-out-of-the-oven snickerdoodles." He presented the table with a flourish of his hand.

"Snickerdoodles?" She slowly swung her legs over the edge of the bed.

"According to Rick, they're your favorite." He walked

over to her and pulled her up to him. "Personally, I don't think anything can compare with this." He began to nibble on her neck.

Suddenly self-conscious, Laurie brought her hand up to cover her mouth. "J.D., don't."

"Ah hah, a case of dragon breath. Never fear. I also purchased a few necessities you forgot yesterday." He let her go and headed her toward the bathroom.

"J.D.!" She couldn't believe it. On the counter top were two toothbrushes, one soft and one hard; three kinds of toothpaste, two bottles of lotion, a packet of razors, four different colors of nail polish, and a very expensive bottle of perfume. "What on earth have you done?"

"Well, I didn't know what you liked so I got one of everything. I hope you like the perfume. I think I smelled every one in the store."

"I'll be right out." Laurie stepped quickly into the bathroom and leaned against the door. How on earth had she been lucky enough to find such a man? Was it possible that her luck was changing? Maybe he would be the one to set her free from the burden of her past. Maybe he would not only understand her past but love her in spite of it. Yeah, and maybe she'd be six feet tall by noon.

She brushed her teeth and slid into the fluffy robe lying across the counter. Anyone this considerate deserved someone without skeletons in their closet.

They ate breakfast over the morning paper and J.D. finally announced he had to leave. "I'll be glad to transfer to the day shift."

"I had completely forgotten you worked all night." She had been so wrapped up in her own dilemma that she really hadn't given much thought to what she had put J.D. through. "You go get some sleep. I have to get to the office and I probably should call Detective

Anderson. The police must have thought I was a lunatic yesterday."

"Sweetheart, you had a perfectly normal reaction to the events of the last few days." He leaned down and placed a kiss on her forehead before heading for the door.

"Call me when you wake up?"

"You shouldn't have to ask that question." His eyes told her all she needed to know.

"Fine. Call me when you wake up," she ordered.

"Yes, dear." He gave her a mock salute and was gone. The room seemed much larger without him.

She placed a call to Detective Anderson and had to listen to his probes and innuendoes. The man had decided she was guilty and nothing seemed to sway him. Basically, he told her he didn't have any leads. He also hinted that it was her fault for not being truthful.

Funny how a person's life could go along smoothly for years and then in the space of a few days . . . A few days. Had it only been such a short time?

She walked over to the dressing table and slid open the drawer. Sure enough, all the usual hotel paraphernalia. The envelopes and brochures she could do without, but the paper would come in handy. As far as the Bible went, she hadn't stopped praying for the last twenty-four hours.

She returned to the table and pushed her breakfast aside. She had work to do.

The best thing for her to do was go back over the last week and try to detect a pattern. Any kind of clue. The list was disturbing. Only two things were out of the ordinary. One, Conway was out of town, so she was in charge of the mall. Was that the connection? Did someone have something against her at work? Was someone out to stop Christmas? Yeah, the grinch. The only other thing that had happened to her was meeting J.D. It couldn't have anything to do with him, could it? Maybe it was like that movie, *Fatal Attraction*. Maybe she had a secret admirer . . . no that wouldn't make sense. An old boyfriend that wanted revenge. Possibly J.D. had an old girlfriend lurking in basements making bombs. It seemed a little far-fetched even in her stressed-out condition.

She continued to review the events of the past few weeks while she dressed in the purple suede dress from Gloria. Her mind was so caught up in her analysis that she failed to notice how stunning she looked. Slipping into the calf-high matching boots she hurried out the door.

Carrie and Frankie tiptoed around her all morning. She knew they were just concerned, but it drove her crazy to be treated like a hot-house flower. She barricaded herself in the office with paperwork. She didn't dare leave and miss her call.

She had almost finished the paperwork for December when it finally came. The message had been simple. Someone was out for her hide. The only person they hadn't been able to clear was J.D. According to them, they had no idea who he was. The file on J.D. Westat began five years ago, before then he didn't exist.

"Let us pick him up," the voice on the other end offered.

"No." She was short and to the point.

"Look, he's got to be the one. Just because you didn't recognize him, doesn't mean he isn't holding some type of a grudge. He could have had plastic surgery. He could be somebody's brother," the voice persuaded. "Any way you look at it, he's bad news. Sounds like you don't need any more of that."

Laurie massaged her temple trying to ward off the headache pounding its way into her brain. "If he is the one, I'll take care of it from this end. Do you understand?"

The phone call was ended and Laurie fought the urge to crawl up in the corner and have a good cry. She knew the information she had just received was correct and she should probably let them handle J.D. She knew a lot of things she should do but wouldn't. Not until J.D. gave her no choice.

This wasn't *Fatal Attraction*, this was *Prizzi's Honor* and she knew how Kathleen Turner must have felt when Jack Nicholson planted a knife in her throat. The only difference was J.D. had stuck her in the heart.

J.D. had gone back to his apartment and forced himself to do a couple loads of laundry. He had to stay away from the mall for a couple of hours so Laurie wouldn't get suspicious.

Clifton's men hadn't turned up anything at the mall. While it was aggravating not to have any leads, J.D. felt vindicated. His mind wasn't so far gone that he was getting careless. He had opened the case file and studied it again now that he was more familiar with the players. Still nothing clicked. He had searched her office and home twice looking for that damned package and hadn't . . . *Package!* Westat, you stupid idiot. What have you been doing for the past few days? Opening packages!

She had to be receiving the packages at the mall. If she received them at home, Pitsie might open one. It wouldn't do for a seventeen year old to open a box containing thousands of dollars. He had been overlooking the obvious from the start. No one at the mall would open a package addressed to Laurie. It was the perfect set-up. Only one way to find out if he was right. Grabbing his jacket, he flew out of his apartment.

Frankie had gone to lunch when he arrived at the mall and he saw no sign of Laurie in the storeroom. Much as he hated it, the more he worked on the idea, the better it seemed to pan out. He had wondered why Laurie was willing to get all sweaty and grimy lugging those crates around. He had never met a woman who would volunteer for a nasty job like that if there was a man around to do it. Still, she had been there everyday, working right along with them. She had to. She was looking for a package containing a rather impressive Christmas bonus.

He discarded the large boxes. Clifton had given him an approximate size, not too large or small. Merely inconspicuous. He picked up a few and tossed them over his shoulder, not caring what damage he might be causing in the process. For thirty minutes he kicked and slung boxes until he found it. Right there in front of him was the proof that would send Laurie to prison.

The mailing label was almost ripped off, but he knew this was the one. He slid his hand into the front pocket of his jeans and struggled to extricate his pocketknife. Flipping open the blade, he carefully slit the paper.

"Oh hear the bells, sweet silver bells . . ."

J.D. barely had time to stuff the box under a Fourth of July decoration before Laurie made it to the room. "You should take it on the road, darlin'."

"J.D.! My gracious, you scared me to death."

"Hey, I was just standing here." Even though he knew she was a criminal, it didn't stop his heart from speeding at the sight of her in that purple dress.

"I thought you were going back to your apartment." Her eyes narrowed with unspoken suspicions. "You must not need much sleep."

J.D. noticed the frost in her voice. "I don't sleep well during the day. I'll catch a few more hours before I go on duty tonight." He quickly stepped over and put his arms around her. "You look gorgeous in that dress." He leaned closer to whisper in her ear. " 'Course you looked pretty fantastic in my shirt, too."

She forced herself from his embrace. "Have you catalogued what you opened?"

He slouched against the wall and studied her. "I just got here."

One look at the dirt covering him and she knew that was a lie. What had he been doing here? Planting another bomb?

"What's the matter?" J.D. straightened up and walked toward her. "You're white as a ghost." He noticed her tense.

"That's ridiculous." Dear Lord, please don't let him be involved.

"You gonna tell me what the hell is goin' on?" His eyes were chips of blue ice and his jaw muscles worked with anger.

"I don't know what you're talking about. I have work to do." She twirled away from him and marched toward the door.

J.D. grabbed her arm and held her fast. "Listen, lady, I was under the impression that we liked, hell, more than liked each other this morning." He forced her to look at him. "What's happened in the last four hours, babe?"

Laurie realized she had better get a grip on her emotions. If she hoped to learn anything about J.D. and his possible involvement, she had better not alienate him. "I'm sorry, I didn't mean to snap."

"Hey, that's okay. If you can't snap at your best fellow, who can you snap at?" He pulled her to him for a quick hug.

"I should get back to the office." She wished he would quit playing with her hair. She wished she would quit liking it.

"Can I buy you lunch before you return to the salt mines?"

Laurie looked into his eyes and knew she would

agree to just about anything he suggested. It was a scary realization.

As they headed for the food court, Laurie noticed Henry as they left the storage room. He was standing in front of the jewelry store looking a little lost. "Hey, good looking, want to have lunch with us?" She could feel J.D. stiffen, but there was safety in numbers.

"Laurie!" Henry looked anything but happy to see her. "I, uh, what did you say?"

"She asked if you'd like to have lunch with us. Or are you meeting a certain beautiful dark-eyed woman?" J.D. was puzzled by the older man's behavior. He was usually overjoyed to see Laurie. Right now Henry looked like he might bolt for the door.

"Oh, thank you, but I've already eaten." Henry glanced around. "Well, I must be off. See you later, Laurie, J.J."

"J.J.?" Laurie stared after Henry. "What's the matter with him. He acted like he just robbed a bank."

"Beats me, but I'm just as glad. I want you all to myself. Besides, Henry treats me like I'm not good enough for you." He led her to Maria's Little Mexico.

"Are you?"

"Probably not." J.D. seated her and went to place their order.

It didn't take long for either one of them to finish their tacos since neither one said a word. Laurie was too caught up in her own thoughts to notice the uncomfortable silence, but J.D. wasn't.

"Laurie, please tell me what's wrong. I'll make it right." He reached across the small table and grabbed her hand. "I'll try to anyway."

One simple sentence that could be interpreted so many ways. Laurie didn't know if it was an act of love or a death threat. J.D. wasn't sure whether he meant to urge a confession out of her or offer to join her organization. The way he felt, both were possibilities.

"Would you?" Laurie let him keep her hand. "Could you?"

J.D. looked into her fathomless green eyes. And told her the truth. "I don't know."

They sat at the table, drinking in the sight of each other. Both terribly afraid that the next few hours might be the last they would ever spend together.

Laurie's beeper went off and the real world intruded. "I need to get back to the office. Carrie and Frankie are still at lunch and with the way things have been going, who knows what this could be about."

"Come on." Laurie didn't protest as he gathered their trash and followed her. A few more minutes of happiness couldn't hurt.

Those minutes turned to seconds as Laurie unlocked the office door. "I must be hallucinating. Tell me I've lost my mind and this office doesn't look like it's been in a food processor."

"Don't touch anything." J.D.'s voice was very official. "The police will want to see it just like this."

"Why? So they can check for prints?" Her voice was high-pitched and strained. "You know there won't be any prints. Just like there weren't any on the bomb or in my house. Whoever is doing this is too professional to be that sloppy."

"Laurie." J.D. tried to soothe her.

"Laurie what! Laurie, you're crazy! Laurie, someone isn't out to get you?" Her eyes blazed, daring him to tell her. "Just what is it you think needs to be said?"

"I'd like to tell you to calm down, but I don't see that happening in the near future." He returned her fury. "Do you want to come with me while I call Detective Anderson or not?"

"Why not call him from here? You know as well as I

do that anyone professional enough to pick this lock and trash the place in less than an hour didn't leave any stupid fingerprints." She stalked to the phone and pressed the numbers. "This is Laurie Morrison at Westwind Mall. Send Detective Anderson and Officer Morton over. I've been hit again." She didn't feel the need to elaborate and hung up. "J.D., what is going on? My life was perfectly normal, blissfully dull until a week ago when you showed up."

J.D. gaped at her. Was she accusing him?

"J.D., I don't care what kind of game you're playing, I want it stopped. You just said you would make everything all right." She shook her finger in his face. "Okay, big shot, do it! If you want to take me out then do it, but leave my family and friends the hell alone!" Realizing she had said too much, she pushed past him and ran down the hallway. Frankie met her at the door and she explained what had happened. "I'm sorry, Frankie, but I just can't deal with it right now." She flew across the mall. She had to go home and try to salvage what was left of her life.

EIGHT

"I don't wanna do this," Pitsie whined. She gingerly placed one sneaker clad foot on the bottom step of the porch.

"I know, sweetie, but it has to be done. If we want to get any insurance money, we have to go through the house." She had contacted her insurance agent and he had promised to do his best. Unfortunately, nothing could be done until the police had finished their investigation.

"Couldn't we just hire somebody to do it?" Pitsie refused to venture any closer. Her blonde hair was tied into a knot on top of her head and a bright neon scarf hung in her eyes.

Laurie reached over and pushed the scarf back. "We will hire a cleaning agency for the biggest part, but I think it'll be good for both of us to face this thing. There are some of our things that I just don't trust to anyone else. Pitsie," Laurie took Pitsie's hand. "We can't let these jerks control our lives. People who do things like this thrive on the fear of others. Do you want to give them that satisfaction?"

"No." Pitsie still didn't sound convinced. Maybe it

was a mistake to make her face the remains of their memories. Laurie had called her friend Kathy this morning to be sure.

Kathy was a trained psychologist who dealt with crime victims. She had encouraged Laurie to do this. "Be careful not to push too hard. She has to face this tragedy or it may dominate a great deal of the rest of her life. Take her to the house. She'll balk at first, but try to convince her. If you can't, call me and I'll make room for her on Friday." Kathy was very clear on one point. "You both have to deal with this soon, before it has time to fester in your brains."

Laurie knew just how quickly tragedy could take over your life and color your thoughts and feelings. It had taken her years to escape the shadow of her younger life. She knew what it was like to wake in a cold sweat from the nightmares. To automatically suspect everyone you met. For almost six years she had worked to overcome the crippling effects of being a victim and she would be hanged before she let Pitsie go through that.

"Okay. Here it is in a nutshell. Either you come in and start facing this now or you go to see Kathy on Friday. But, I am here to tell you, you will face it and you will put it behind you." Laurie tried to keep her voice firm. "The thing is, I need you. I don't want to go in there alone."

"Are you scared?" Pitsie sounded as if the very idea was impossible.

"You bet I'm scared. I'm also extremely angry."

"Me, too." Pitsie squeezed her hand and stepped up to the door. "Let's go, sis."

The police had taped a neon yellow strip across the door, indicating a crime scene and Laurie reached up and tore it off. The door creaked open and the smell of rotting food made Laurie gag. "Whew. I forgot about the food."

"Gross." Pitsie reached her fingers up and clamped them on the bridge of her nose. "I think this is one of those things we can let somebody else handle. I'm not exactly sentimental about the roast."

Laurie agreed and they scooted through the kitchen and shut the door behind them. The living and dining rooms were in shambles. Miraculously, a few things remained unscathed. "Pitsie, you clear out a corner and we'll put everything we can salvage in one place. Then we can box it up and I'll take it back to the mall."

It didn't take long to sift through the broken bits of their lives and when Laurie glanced in the corner, the pile was dismally small. Pitsie had already started on her bedroom, so Laurie decided to bring up their luggage and some boxes from the cellar.

The single, bare bulb cast eerie shadows across the jumbled mass in the cellar and Laurie carefully stepped around broken Christmas ornaments and shattered canning jars. The meat in the freezer wasn't quite as rank as that upstairs due to the coolness of the cellar, but the smell was breathtaking.

Most of the boxes she had saved were crushed or soggy with molding canned vegetables. Luckily her luggage remained intact. She grabbed what she could and lugged it up the stairs. The locks had been broken on most of them but at least they still closed. She braved the cellar one more time to haul up her mother's trunk.

The lid had been thrown open and most of the contents were scattered on the floor. She scooped them back into the trunk and hooked the latch. Remembering to lift with her legs, she squatted down to lift the trunk. It was heavier than she had first thought and once she had it halfway up, it pitched forward into the cinderblock wall. Grasping the outer handles she tried again. This time she succeeded in crashing herself into the wall.

Exhausted, she slid down the rough cool wall to the floor. Her jacket hung on the corner of a cinderblock that wasn't flush with the rest and she almost wept when she heard the material rip. "Great."

Letting go of the trunk, she turned around to inspect the wall. No wonder. The trunk must have knocked the brick loose. She almost pulled the block the rest of the way out but decided with her luck, the wall would fall like a card house. She tried shoving it back in, but it was hung up on something. Laurie inched the block out, listening for any noise that might signal collapse. The block came out freely and the wall stood. Cringing at the thought of what might lie in the dark, damp hole in the wall, she reached down and grabbed an old clothes hanger to scrape out the interior. "Oh, my gosh."

With thoughts of aged and brittle paper inscribed with quill pens, she gingerly picked up the pile of letters. A frown wrinkled her brow as she realized the letters weren't old at all.

The letters weren't in their envelopes, but it didn't take her long to discover who they were from. "Nick Davidson, you cradle-robbing scum."

Her brother had brought Nick home with him the last time he had been on leave. Pitsie had, of course, fallen head over heels for the dark, brooding young man. He hadn't given her the time of day, or so Laurie had thought. Obviously he had given her something. Each letter was filled with promises. Promises Laurie was sure he had no intention of honoring. He was at least ten years older than Pitsie, almost Laurie's age. In fact, he had made no secret of the fact that he wasn't at all worried about the two years separating them. Laurie had been forced to turn him down several times before he finally got the message.

Apparently he had turned his attention to Pitsie. The letters made mention of a grandmother, asking Pitsie to check on her and visit with her. He even mentioned how much his grandmother appreciated the times Pitsie came to visit. He commented on the fact that his grandmother was worried about the relationship between them.

"Darling, you must win her over to our side. Take her the presents I send and just listen when she drones on. If we are to be married while I'm still stationed here, you can't live with me and I'll want you to take care of her. She's a tough old boot and she'll turn you against me if she can. Be strong, my love."

Laurie's temper was skyrocketing by the time she'd read that letter. Granted, she had invaded Pitsie's privacy, but if this was the way Pitsie had been acting, she didn't deserve any. Leaving the trunk in the cellar, she stomped up the stairs, bellowing for her sister.

"Care to explain this?" She waved the letters in front of Pitsie.

"Those are mine! You had no right!" Pitsie grabbed the letters and searched them frantically. "There's one missing. What did you do with it?"

"I didn't do anything with it, but I know what I'd like to do with all of them."

Pitsie's face crumpled into a mask of rage. "I hate you."

"You've been lying to me for the past six months and you have the nerve to say that." Laurie felt tears well up behind her eyes. "I just don't understand. I had hoped you were more mature than that."

"I am more mature. Nick's love has done that for me." Pitsie was defiant.

"Nick's love," Laurie spat out. "In a pig's eye. Sweetie, he doesn't mean what he says. He's off on that island and he feels lonely. You don't think you're the only girl he's got writing to him, do you?"

"You don't know what you're talking about. You're just jealous because you wanted him and he wouldn't even look at you." Mascara streaked her face.

"What!"

"Nick told me how you threw yourself at him. He said he felt sorry for you, but once he had seen me he knew I was the only one for him." Her eyes held Laurie's triumphantly.

She tried, but Laurie couldn't help the giggle that broke free. "You actually believe that. Pitsie, I saw Nick Davidson for the greasy little manipulator he was. But that's beside the point. The real issue here is why you felt you had to lie to me."

"You would never understand. Nick says there is something wrong with you. He says you hate men and couldn't understand what we have. His grandmother at least gives me some credit."

"Pitsie, I am perfectly aware of what Nick thinks of me." She indicated the letters clasped to Pitsie's chest. "However, what I'm worried about is what has happened to us. I wouldn't have stopped you from writing Nick. I would just hope you would keep things in perspective. Nick is a grown man, and for all your big talk you are still pretty young." Laurie tried to remain calm and reasonable. "I know it's hard, honey, but you have to face the facts. If Nick really cared for you, and if you were really sure of your love for him, then you wouldn't be playing these childish games. Adults don't hide their feelings."

"You do," Pitsie accused.

"What are you talking about?"

"Anyone can look at you and J.D. and see you're in love with him. Have you told him?"

Laurie held her breath. "Pitsie, that's different." Was it?

"How?"

"I haven't known J.D. very long. He knows that I have feelings for him, but even I'm not sure that I love him. It could just be a healthy case of lust."

Pitsie shrugged her shoulders. "So sleep with him."

"Pitsie!"

"I thought all adults slept together." Laurie could tell she was baiting her. Boy, was she glad she could deny sleeping with J.D. Still, if she had had her way this morning . . .

"Maybe some adults do. But that isn't the way to deal with everything. Especially not in this day and age." Laurie stepped closer to Pitsie. "But whether or not I've made love with J.D. isn't what we're discussing. I need to know what we're going to do about Nick."

Pitsie's chin shot up. "I'm gonna marry him. The day I turn eighteen."

"Fine. If you and he both want that, the day you turn eighteen you go right ahead. Until then, since I really don't have a lot of faith in your judgment or truthfulness right now, we're going to have to rethink the rules."

"You can't tell me what to think, or feel, or even what to do. I can do whatever I want. And right now, I want to get as far away from you as possible." Pitsie searched Laurie's face for the effect her words had on her sister. "I'm going to Nick's grandmother's. She may think I'm too young for Nick, but at least she doesn't act like I'm an idiot." Pitsie fled the room and Laurie had to check herself before she tackled her. Her emotions were to close to the surface right now and she had let her tongue run wild. She had really messed up. She and Pitsie both needed to cool off before anything could be resolved. She forced herself to finish sorting through the debris before returning to the office.

She would have to face what had happened there, too. Just as she would have to face J.D. Pitsie was right, she did love him.

running to the store for a gallon of milk. He needed to

NINE

J.D. had stayed to help Frankie and Carrie restore the office to some semblance of order before he headed back to the storeroom and the little brown package.

He had to practically lay on the floor to retrieve it from its hiding place. He took his time examining it. There was no room for error. The first thing he noticed was the zip code on the mailing label was not the one used for the mall. It was, however, the one used for Laurie's home address. Therefore, he deduced, it might have been sent to her home. Throwing caution to the wind, he removed the solid brown paper.

He found two boxes wrapped in bright Christmas paper and a letter.

Sweetheart,
 Here is your present and one for Grandmother. I know you will see she gets it. I feel she is coming around to our way of thinking. Soon we'll be able to tell everyone. The whole world! Please tell Grandmother that I am keeping busy and I will be seeing you both sooner than I thought. Hope you like your gift.

                      Love,
                      Nick

J.D. would have laughed if it wasn't so incredible. He had expected to find thousands of untraceable dollars. Instead he found Christmas presents. Clifton had assured him that Davidson was passing large amounts of money to Laurie on a regular basis. J.D. shook his head, this whole affair was too unbelievable. His keen analytical mind couldn't get a handle on it. That in itself was highly unusual. But this assignment was far from the neat little package he had expected.

He went over the missing links in his mind. First, if Laurie was so hot for Davidson, why was she so responsive to him? Acting? Second, who was this grandmother? Clifton hadn't mentioned Davidson having any relatives in Amarillo. It was possible she didn't even factor into the equation. Third, if this guy wasn't shipping anything but presents then why had Laurie's home and office been trashed? He didn't buy Clifton's theory that she was trying to throw suspicion off her. That was too amateur. The searches had been thorough and vicious. He glanced at the presents in his hands and decided what the heck. Carefully peeling back the tape, he opened Laurie's present.

"What in the world is this?" The box contained a pair of the most hideously gawdy earrings he had ever laid eyes on. Laurie wouldn't be caught dead in anything like these. Pitsie maybe.

He retaped the paper carefully. Maybe no one would notice. Then he started on the larger box. "Great Scott!"

Either the Marines were paying a heck of a lot better than when he was in the Corps, or Nick was supplementing his paycheck. Granny's present was an intricately carved cameo jewelry box. That in itself wasn't too bad, but the tight little stacks of money inside could sure keep an old lady warm on a Panhandle night.

The relief that coursed through him was immediate and gratifying. If Laurie was to deliver this to Nick's grandmother, that meant she wasn't really too involved. Certainly not the boss lady. More than likely, Nick was skimming off the terrorists' payroll and shipping it home to dear old Granny.

Clifton would have a coronary when J.D. reported this one. If Davidson had gotten Laurie involved, it was on a very small level. Shoot, the poor girl was probably innocent.

He rewrapped the entire package and placed it back among the unopened boxes. He had a busy night ahead of him if he wanted to get this mess wrapped up. Clifton had gotten hold of some misinformation. Nick was involved with the organization, but he wasn't any underground hero out to stop the bad guys. He was sticking Laurie, not to mention his own grandmother, in a potentially explosive situation while he sat protected on a U.S. Marine base. He hadn't heard of any other houses in town being trashed, so maybe whoever was after this little package didn't know about the grandmother. He would have Clifton stick a couple of men on her. He didn't like the idea of anyone's grandmother having to go through what Laurie was suffering.

If he had anything to say about it, Laurie was out of it, too. He quickly scanned the room and made a mental list of what he required. Luckily he would be alone at the mall all night. Plenty of time to get his equipment in place. Now he had to call Clifton, and then find a way to convince Laurie he was one of the good guys.

Laurie was amazed at how quickly she had been able to finish compiling her list for the insurance. Donald had been clearly shocked at the wreckage and promised to do his best for her.

Of equal astonishment was the fact that Carrie and Frankie had managed to clear up the office in the few hours she had been gone. When Frankie explained that J.D. had willingly answered all of Detective Anderson's questions and stuck around to help, her heart sang. If he was willing to work with the police, he must not be hiding anything too incriminating. Unless his new personality and cover were foolproof. And Laurie knew there was no way any cover was foolproof. There were flaws in every system. If J.D. wasn't avoiding the police, it was possible he was in the government's eye-witness program. That would certainly explain why J.D. Westat hadn't existed five years ago. Why her contacts had no record of the change.

Laurie mechanically stripped off her coat and gloves. Her snow boots were making puddles on the entry mat. By the time she had headed back to the office the snow had really started coming down. Luckily, most of the stores were closing early for the holiday and wouldn't open until Friday morning. Since Pitsie was determined to stay with Nick's grandmother, Laurie was alone. Frankie had left her a list of details to be taken care of before Santa's arrival on Friday. His crew had finished hanging the last of the decorations before they left and Laurie only had to decorate the huge tree gracing the commons area. She thought of the dozens of crushed ornaments in her cellar and fought back the tears. Some of them had been in her family for generations. She renewed her vow to find the jerks who had done this to her.

Rick had hand delivered a jumbo Dr. Pepper and a dozen cookies before he left for the holiday. "Don't worry, I'm not that generous. They'd be stale before Friday."

She checked her messages and noticed that there was one from Nick's grandmother. She had left her phone number so Laurie quickly punched out the numbers.

"May I speak to Pitsie, this is her sister."

"Oh my dear, I can't tell you how grateful I am that you have allowed Pitsie to be with me for Thanksgiving. With Nick off on that island, I am so alone. I want you to know you are welcome, too. Pitsie explained that you already had plans and that was why you allowed her to accept my invitation."

Any protest she might have made died in Laurie's throat. Why hadn't Pitsie told her the woman had invited her. Probably because you were ranting and raving at each other. "Could I speak to Pitsie?"

"Certainly, child."

Pitsie was still pouting when she answered the phone and Laurie assured her that her big sister wasn't such an ogre. "I know we weren't exactly having a normal conversation, but I wouldn't make you leave her all alone on Thanksgiving."

"Thanks, Laurie, and I'm sorry that I kept Nick a secret. I'm really glad you know about it now. You don't want to come over tomorrow, do you?" She didn't sound very encouraging.

"No. I think I'll take your advice and tell J.D. how I feel. If all goes right, I'll have lunch with him."

"Go for it." Pitsie hung up before Laurie could get an address.

Grabbing her drink and cookies, she headed for the commons area and the waiting tree. Most of the lights were out and it was already dark outside. Frankie had thoughtfully provided a battery operated spot light to shine on the tree. Stepping inside the protective fencing, she got down to business. If she could finish this quickly, she would have time to talk to J.D. when he came on duty.

An hour later she stood back and surveyed her handiwork. "Not bad. Not bad at all."

The tree twinkled with hundreds of multicolored lights

and the enormous glass ornaments reflected their glow. Tiny angels danced on the branches and Laurie especially liked the new Disney ornaments. She hoped they wouldn't lose too many of them to theft. Every year they lost a good percentage of their decorations to sneaky fingers.

She spread the bright red felt cloth around the base of the tree and positioned a few "presents" for realism. On Friday, the mall employees would bring their gifts to each other for Santa to hand out. There was also a large box by Santa's chair that held the names of several needy children. Mall patrons were encouraged to choose a child to help over the holidays.

She hooked the fencing together and flipped off the spot light. Immediately she found herself in total darkness. What had happened to the lights? They had been on an hour ago.

She flipped on the spot light and discovered that it only cast a dim glow a few feet wide. The battery was dying—fast. Deciding it would be foolish to wait for J.D. in the dark, she headed for her office. Surely he would find her there.

"Who's there?" Laurie whispered as a loud crash echoed through the darkness. She shone the light in the direction of the noise, but it wasn't bright enough. She glanced at her watch. It wasn't time for J.D. to be on duty. With a surge of fear and anger, she decided she had had enough. Determined, she strode toward the storeroom.

J.D. had finished hooking the last wire to his hidden generator, when he heard the crash. Extinguishing his flashlight, he waited. Someone talking? Slipping behind the large crate he had moved the other day, he concentrated on the noise.

It had been a long time since he had been required to do any actual physical fighting, other than with Laurie, but he tried to stay in shape. Besides, his uniform came well equipped. He flicked open his holster in readiness.

Someone was coming. Soft, careful steps designed not to be heard. Tensed, J.D. felt pricks along his spine as he sprang into action. "Freeze!"

Instinctively, Laurie dropped to the floor and rolled. J.D. flung himself on top of her. "I said freeze."

Laurie froze as the metal of his gun planted itself against her temple. "What do you want?"

"Laurie?" J.D. eased the gun away from her head and released the hammer.

"You scared the pants off me," Laurie said, struggling into a sitting position. J.D. still straddled her legs.

"You didn't do a whole lot for me either, lady." He slid his gun back into its holster and pulled her against him. "What were you doing sneaking around in the dark like that? I could have shot you!"

Laurie recognized the terror behind his anger and took comfort in it. "I'm in the dark because we've lost the power, and I was sneaking because I hoped to catch whoever was fooling around in here."

"Great. I guess I'm lucky you don't carry a gun or I'd probably be decorating the back wall."

Laurie surreptitiously slid her switchblade into her back pocket. She'd rather J.D. not know how close he had come to finding it in his chest. "J.D., I'm sorry about razing you earlier. I plead temporary insanity."

J.D. stroked her hair and squeezed her tighter. He was still shaking inside at the thought of his gun against her soft skin. He had surely bruised her at the very least. He felt sick that he had hurt her in any way. "I . . ."

Laurie placed her finger over his lips. "Shush, I'm just fine. You were only doing your job, and with all that's been going on lately, who could blame us for being jumpy?"

"What are you doing here at this time of night?" He kissed her finger before she moved it.

"I could ask you the same thing. You don't go on duty for another hour." She went on to explain about Pitsie staying with her boyfriend's grandmother for the holiday and of her determination to get everything ready for Friday. "I was planning to invite you to join me for lunch at the hotel."

J.D. could feel her heart pounding and he knew what it must have cost her to ask him that. She still wasn't sure of him, but she was willing to put forth the effort. Guess Davidson wasn't the love of her life after all.

"I'd love to, but right now I'm escorting you to your car so you can go back to the hotel." He helped her to her feet and kissed her briefly.

"Aw, do I have to?"

"Yes, you do, young lady." They wrapped their arms around each other as they headed for her office. Laurie had to stretch her steps to match his.

"J.D., look!" Laurie skidded to a stop pulling him back.

"What is it, darlin'?" He peered in the direction of the large glass doors at the mall's entrance. "Whew."

"That's an understatement. That is a full-fledged Texas Panhandle blizzard." Laurie walked over to the door and pressed her face against it. "I can't see anything."

"You can't go anywhere either." J.D. had come up behind her. He pulled her back against him, and except for the gun poking into her side, it felt wonderful. She had debated, and pondered, and prayed all day about her decision to tell J.D. she was in love with him. If he was the kind of man she suspected, there would be a great deal of responsibility in admitting that. He would want her to take an active part in their relationship. She felt she could handle the physical part of any relationship with J.D., but she was a little worried about the complete honesty he would demand from her.

"Guess you're stuck with me." She turned and pressed her face to his chest. "At least we'll be safe. If we can't get out, no one can get in." Laurie took his hand and led him in the direction of her office and the extra long couch in Frankie's office. She was officially taking him off duty.

TEN

J.D. helped himself to the last of her cookies and one of Frankie's Mexican beers. Laurie had turned up her nose when he tried to kiss her and he had thoughtfully chewed a stick of gum.

"Better?" He blew a breath in her face.

"Well, you pass the smell test, but I don't know about the taste test," she teased as he pulled her closer on the big couch.

"Oh, you haven't taken our taste test, miss? Well, here we have sample number one." He placed light kisses on each eyelid. "To be fair, you have to close your eyes. Now, ready?" Laurie nodded her head and J.D placed a gentle kiss on her lips. "Now please leave your eyes closed for sample number two."

This kiss didn't tease, it tortured. Laurie's senses were reeling and she willingly lay back on the couch, pulling him with her. "I can't make up my mind, could I try number two again?"

J.D. growled and plunged his tongue into her seeking mouth. Only when he had satisfied himself with her lips did he move his mouth along her jaw and down her neck. Shockwaves coursed through her. She wanted to give back the same pleasures she was receiving, but due to the course J.D. was taking, she could only reach the top of his head.

Her fingers forced their way past the buttons of his shirt and curled in the fine sprinkling of hair along the center of his chest. Her nail skimmed over his flat male nipple and his groan was pure animal. Testing her feminine powers, she scraped the tender flesh once more and J.D. surged upward, taking her mouth again.

Laurie knew that if she allowed him a moment to think, he would stop then and she didn't want that. She slid her legs around him and locked him to her. It didn't seem to matter that he was a foot taller. In this ancient position, they were equal.

They fit together perfectly. She felt small and dainty lying under him. She knew this was where she belonged and that this was the man to slay her dragons.

She could feel her body readying itself for him. This in itself was a new experience. Anytime she had tried to be intimate with a man her body had betrayed her and made it impossible. With J.D. her body was ready without any encouragement from her.

J.D. traced the curve of her ear with his tongue and she couldn't think anymore. Hands fumbled and clothing flew. Flesh met flesh and it was heaven. Her lacey bra was flung through the air and landed on the other side of the room.

J.D. trailed his mouth downward, seeking her breast and Laurie had to restrain herself from pushing him faster. She could feel the heat of his breath on the sensitive flesh. She waited for him to taste her there. Ached for it. What was wrong? Did he think she was deformed? She knew her left breast was smaller than her right breast, but she had never thought it would turn someone off. She opened her eyes and tried to focus in the darkness. J.D. had lifted himself partially off of her and was listening. "What's wrong?"

"Do you smell something?" he whispered.

"What?" She couldn't believe her ears.

J.D. sprang up and reached for the gun he had placed on the floor. Laurie sat up and covered herself with her hands. Great! Why was it always the woman who was left half-naked and vulnerable? Just once she'd like to see a man running around with his . . . his . . . self hanging out.

"J.D., this is ridiculous . . ."

He cut her off. "Laurie, I smell gas or something."

Laurie tilted her button nose at the vaguely familiar stench. She found her blouse and shrugged into it, buttoning the tiny buttons with shaking fingers. J.D. had opened the door of Frankie's office and the pungent odor was much stronger. She walked to the doorway and sniffed.

"I hear something in my office." She cocked her head at the spewing noise.

"Stay back," J.D. ordered and walked across the lobby to her office. Suddenly Laurie recognized the deadly odor of chlorine gas.

"J.D., stop!"

Laurie watched horrified as J.D. wrenched open her office door and felt the brunt of the gas. Instantly, Laurie plunged across the lobby and tackled J.D., flinging him free of the deadly gas billowing from her office. Burying her face against him to keep the gas from burning her eyes and scorching its way down her lungs, she helped him stumble from the office suite into the hallway.

J.D. lay on the floor gasping for air, tears streamed from his eyes. Laurie struggled to get him back on his feet and further away from the office.

She knew he desperately needed oxygen. She thought

of the bottle stashed behind Frankie's desk for emergencies but it would be suicide for her to try and retrieve it. There was no way she could cover herself sufficiently to protect the delicate membranes of her nose and throat from the invisible gas. "J.D., I've got to get to the food court. They keep a bottle of oxygen down there and you need it."

Without waiting for a reply she flew across the mall, shrieking in pain as she ran into the jewelry kiosk in the dark. Fighting the urge to inch along in the darkness, she kept on running. The gas had only had a few seconds to work on J.D., but he still needed oxygen.

Calling herself a fool for not having a flashlight, she finally managed to locate the storage closet next to the restrooms. It was locked, but a few well-placed kicks on the knob bent the lock enough for her to pry it open. Fumbling on the shelves she managed to find a flashlight that mercifully worked. Shining it on the interior of the closet she found the green tank and hoisted it on her shoulder.

The trip back to J.D. was much easier with the flashlight, but the sight of him wrenched her heart. She didn't stop to wonder about the implications of an open bottle of chlorine gas in her office.

J.D. gratefully pressed the mouthpiece over his face and breathed in the rich oxygen between coughs. Laurie wiped his face with the edge of her shirt until he pushed her hand away. "I'm okay."

"Me, too," she answered his unspoken question. "Keep that on your face."

"You should take some." He struggled to sit up.

She shook her head. "As soon as I recognized the chlorine I held my breath. You protected me."

"From whom? That's what I'd like to know." He grabbed her hand. "Babe, what's going on? This is no joke, no warning. If you had opened that door you might have passed out before you could get away. You would have been dead in a matter of seconds."

"J.D.!" She turned wide eyes to him. He saw the panic tinging their green depths. "There has to be someone else in the mall."

"Damn." His brain was still so fuddled he couldn't think straight. Laurie was right. Someone had come into the office while they were in Frankie's office and opened a pressurized bottle of chlorine gas. "Someone is getting good at sending you messages."

"What do you mean me? Couldn't they be sending them to you?" The panic was replaced by anger. "I mean, nothing ever happened to me until you showed up."

"Okay, I'll concede it could be me, but I doubt it. My apartment hasn't been searched, and it was your office that was just perfumed," he pointed out bluntly.

"I don't know what's going on," she conceded. "But, I . . ." She needed to tell him. Needed to trust him. If he wasn't the one after her, and she didn't see how he could be, he might be able to help.

"Yeah?" He slipped the clear plastic mask off his face and shifted to look at her. He could see she was nervous even in the dim light.

"There's probably something you should know about me. If you don't already." She switched off the light and leaned back against the wall. She had buried her secret so deep within her for so long, she wasn't sure she could find the words to tell him.

"I know I love you." He realized that was the truth and no matter what she was about to tell him, he had to say those words to her first. He would tell her again after.

"Oh, J.D., I wish you wouldn't say things like that. It just makes this harder." She felt his hand slip over hers and she took a deep fortifying breath.

"When I was seventeen I enlisted in the Navy. You know, sort of following in the old man's footsteps. Anyway, after I had been in a couple of years, N.I. approached me. I had never thought about Intelligence being part of my career, but they seemed to think I had what it took." She closed her eyes against the threatening pain. "My dad was skeptical, but I saw it as a terrific way to serve my country and further my career."

She paused a moment and glanced at J.D. His eyes were closed and he didn't seem to have anything to say. "At first it was dead boring. I was shifted to tiny offices all over the world doing mainly clerical work. I worked for some of the best in the business and learned anything and everything they were willing to teach. After a few months I started routine surveillance. I learned disguises, voice techniques, the works. I realize a lot of this doesn't make any sense to you, but just hear me out." She touched J.D.'s lips as he started to speak.

"I became more valuable and much more sophisticated. I was used to ferret our male counter-agents or terrorists. It seems I have a knack for stringing men along." Her laugh was grating and bitter. "Well anyway, let's just say I do have my share of enemies, so you're probably right. The messages are mine."

"Any idea who it could be?"

"None. I left the Navy five years ago and I haven't heard or seen anything like active duty since."

"What about lately?" It was a risk he decided to take. He was mad enough to spit nails. Clifton had played him for a fool.

"I told you, nothing."

"Babe, are you telling me that you have no connection with anyone at all?"

"I think you'd better explain." Her voice was suspicious.

"Laurie, you're not gonna like this." Boy, was that an understatement. "You've been under surveillance for the last week as the head of a terrorist organization." He gripped her fingers tightly. "You have received packages and letters from one of the men linked to the organization. Are you sure you don't want to tell me about it?"

"FBI or CIA?"

He didn't even pretend not to understand. "I'm with an organization called Technical Anti-Terrorism force. TAT for short. Until a week ago I was semi-retired."

"You rat!" She wrenched her hand from his grasp and spun away.

"Yeah, I know." His gut ached. "Babe, you know how it is. They tell you to do it and you do it. Remember," he forced her to face him, "last week I didn't know you from Adam. If I really believed you were the head of a bunch of fanatics, do you think I'd be tellin' you all this?" He tried to force her to look at him, but she refused.

"Don't touch me." The words were barely a whisper.

He removed his hands and held them up. "Okay, just hear me out." He shifted so that he was leaning back against the wall, his arm pressed to hers. "Several things have helped build a case against you. I hope you can remember what it's like to be on assignment and not pass judgment."

Anger radiated from her. "I assume you mean don't be mad because you've gone through my life with a fine toothed comb?"

"Evidently not or I would have been aware of your Navy background."

"How could you not know! I'm sure you have a complete dossier." The bitterness in her voice stung worse than the gas.

"I plan on finding out how that was skipped over,

but I promise it was not in your file. I'll even show you the darn thing if we ever get out of here." He slammed a clenched fist against his thigh. "It sure as hell would have explained a lot."

Laurie shot him a look at his choice of words, but decided now was not the time for a language lesson. "Such as?"

"Such as the fact that you are obviously an expert at defending yourself. I didn't believe for a minute that you had picked up moves like that at the local YMCA. I knew you had to have been extensively trained. You were too controlled, too professional. I tried to convince Clifton he had the wrong person, but then I found those letters in your basement."

"You slime!" Her hand connected with his cheek and J.D. actually saw stars. "How could you have done that to my home?"

He grabbed her wrist before she could inflict any further damage. "I asked you to hear me out! No, I didn't trash your house or your office, and according to Clifton neither did anyone else from the agency. That's part of the reason I began to suspect you weren't our suspect. Clifton tried to convince me that it was all a clever ruse to hide your involvement. He also tried to convince me that you'd stop at nothing to protect your comrades." His meaning was crystal clear. Whoever this Clifton was had thought her low enough to sleep with J.D. to protect whatever secrets she had.

"Nice guy," she mumbled.

"Look, I said I don't believe you're the head."

"But you do think I'm involved. You don't have any idea how wrong you are." She drew in a harsh, hurting breath. "J.D., I can't abide killing. That's why I was no good at the spy game anymore. After what happened, I . . ."

J.D. wanted her to go on, to tell him what had turned

her life upside-down, but she clammed up. "Apparently I don't know anything about you. I hope you'll tell me when all this is over."

"When will that be? It could have been tonight."

J.D. decided to forego the rest of their true confessions and concentrate on the problem at hand. He knew there was a screw-up in the information chain and Laurie was in real danger. There was someone in the mall with them. He had already struck once and the night was still young. "Laurie, we need to find a place that's easily defendable. Someplace we can see them coming."

"Them?"

"Whoever's running this search and destroy mission. Come on, don't blank out on me now. I need a trained mind if we're gonna see tomorrow."

"Right. It's just that I'm not entirely sure who to trust right now." Laurie had led J.D. to the food court and they settled on the ladies' restroom. It had two doors and they could each guard one. J.D. would have preferred only one door, but Laurie had argued they might need an escape route. Seeing the set of her determined chin, he had relented.

The bathroom tile was cold and hard so Laurie felt sure she wouldn't be tempted to fall asleep. It had been a long time since she had been in this position. She sat in the dark, listening to every noise and working the new knowledge through the gamut of her logical brain. She sat there for hours before she realized what J.D. had said. Letters!

ELEVEN

"J.D." Laurie's whisper resounded off the tiled walls. She abandoned her post and crawled over to him.

"What's wrong?" He sat up straight and went on full alert. "Did you hear something?"

"No, I just remembered something." She couldn't determine his exact location in the inky darkness and she hoped she wasn't headed for one of the stalls. "Turn on your light a minute." He could hear her coming toward him. "Just keep talking, I'll direct you."

"Great. Just don't run me into the wall." She reached out a hand to test her bearings and felt his fingers sweeping the air.

"Gotcha." J.D. pulled her to him and she half sat on his lap. "Did you miss me?"

"Oh, good grief, save me from your incredible ego." She slid off his lap onto the floor. "J.D., what did you say about finding some letters."

"I already said I didn't trash your house. I left it in perfect condition, even your underwear."

"My underwear! You slime, I can't believe you—no, you're getting me off track. I understand about the search. I realize it was only standard, but what did you say about the letters?"

"I found some letters behind a cinderblock in the cellar. I'm sorry, honey, but your boyfriend is a real bas . . . uh, jerk."

"But he isn't." Laurie shook her head trying to piece this new information into the puzzle.

"Excuse me, lady, but any guy who would involve an innocent lady in international killings is a jerk." He couldn't believe she was defending the creep. Did she love the guy that much?

"No, no, I meant he isn't my boyfriend. He's Pitsie's." Good grief, Nick had been using Pitsie all right, but it was far worse that anything she had imagined. "She's madly in love with him and thinks he's going to marry her."

The rush of relief J.D. felt was overwhelming. He wanted to shout and dance in the streets. She was innocent. Good old instincts, they had come through again!

"How did she meet him?"

"My brother is stationed in Cuba. Nick came home with him last summer. He hit on me for a week before he finally realized I wasn't interested. I noticed Pitsie following him around like a puppy, but he didn't seem to pay her any attention."

J.D. rubbed his forehead. "Has she received any packages from him?"

"Not that I know of. I didn't even know about the letters. Pitsie always gets home first, so she would have time to hide any packages." Laurie laid her head against his shoulder, drawing on his strength. "I feel like such a fool."

"Don't. Nick's smarter than anyone gave him credit for. He convinced Pitsie not to let you know anything about them. She's at that rebellious age." J.D. gave her a quick hug and sprang to his feet. "It's almost morning; if our friend had anything else planned, he would have tried it by now."

Laurie rose beside him and they cautiously opened the door. The sun was just stealing over the horizon and, thankfully, the electricity was back on. J.D. motioned Laurie to trail him and they made their way back toward her office. The chlorine gas had dissipated enough not to be a threat, but Laurie was grateful the mall would be closed today.

J.D. quickly grabbed her purse and their coats. He needed to find a clean telephone and call Clifton. He wanted some answers. *Now!*

The parking lot was knee-deep in snow drifts and they decided to try walking to the hotel.

"It's times like this I miss a bigger city," Laurie muttered, shuffling beside J.D.

"Why?"

"Taxi cabs on every corner."

J.D. chuckled and curled her arm under his. "I didn't realize you were such a wimp. I could have called for a cab, but it would take an hour before it could get here." He tilted her chin up to meet his gaze. "We Marines always said you Navy guys couldn't hack it."

"Nice try, Westat, but I don't intimidate easily. If you expect me to rise to the bait and valiantly show you for the sexist pig you are, forget it." She sniffed against the cold. "I'll make it to the hotel, but don't for one minute think I'm enjoying this."

"How 'bout this?" J.D. enveloped her and locked his frozen lips to hers. Standing on the street corner kissing this woman had to be one of the craziest, sanest things he had ever done. Laurie snuggled inside his jacket and he stepped down off the curb to even their height a bit.

When the kiss ended, both were considerably warmer.

Tucking her back under his arm, they trooped across the almost deserted Interstate toward her waiting hotel room. J.D. knew he would have to leave her alone while he located a clean line and he didn't like the idea.

Her room was warm and rumpled. She had requested that no maid service her room. He let his gaze flicker over the sheets and for a brief moment fantasized about Laurie in her new black nightie decorating the large bed.

Reining in his much too vivid imagination, he automatically searched the room. No visible bugs, but nowadays that didn't mean much. The newest technology had devised bugs so sensitive you could hear through walls.

He noticed Laurie giving the room a quick once over, too. He had to keep reminding himself that she had gone through basically the same training he had. True, he had been at it longer, but they had both been dormant for five years.

With a quick shake of her head Laurie answered his unspoken question. Nothing had been touched. He crossed the room in two quick strides and gently whispered, "I've got to find a clean line."

Laurie realized that he still suspected they were being monitored so she held her lips close to his ear. "I'm worried about a leak."

J.D. nodded. The thought of someone on the inside being responsible for his wild goose chase had also occurred to him.

Although Laurie's Intelligence background would have been buried, her Naval career wouldn't. He would have to feel Clifton out and go with his instincts. They had been right so far. He gave her a quick peck on the cheek and was out the door. He fought the comfortable feeling of domesticity. He could have been a husband running to the store for a gallon of milk. He needed to be away from her for a few minutes to get his act together. Even if she did have special training, he needed to keep his wits about him if they planned on getting out of this alive.

Laurie hurriedly undressed and jumped in the shower. She felt like death warmed over. A night spent sitting in the ladies' room had made her sore everywhere. The hot water sluiced over her and she rotated her head under the hard spray, searching for relief for her aching neck muscles.

She washed her hair twice and then applied conditioner. Since she had quit lightening her hair she rarely had to use a conditioner to keep it healthy, but she felt the need to be pampered, even in this small way.

Rubbing her hand over her shin, she determined a shave was essential. She hated shaving her legs in the shower, but it would be worse to rub her prickly legs over J.D.'s . . . Stop that! The man was strictly off-limits. He was on assignment. A man with a mission that had nothing to do with getting involved.

At the most his involvement with her was temporary. Funny, she had decided five years ago that "temporary" was the only thing she had to offer a man. But then she hadn't been in love before either. There was no doubt in her mind that the gnawing ache within her was the beginning of a very powerful love for J.D. Her body screamed with feelings she had never encountered. Her mind was bogged down with impossible plans of a future with him. No, her time with him might be temporary, but the hurt she would suffer when he left wouldn't be anything close to temporary.

The clanging of the phone cut into her martyrdom. J.D. must have already found the information he needed. Grabbing a towel, she ran to the phone. "Hello?"

"I hope I didn't interrupt anything." The voice was a harsh whisper.

"No." She knew immediately that the voice wasn't J.D. "Who is this?"

"Well, I'll tell you. I believe in operating on a 'need-to-know' basis. As of this moment, you do not need to know." The smugness was easily transmitted.

"Look, buddy, I don't have time for you to play 'big bad boy,' so buzz off." Laurie started to hang up the phone.

"Laurie dear, such poor phone etiquette. What would your dear, departed mother say?" The smugness was gone.

"Who is this?" Anger flushed her face.

"Now, now." The voice paused to make sure his meaning was clear. "All you need to know is that I am presently in a position of some control. You have something I want and I am interested in a little negotiating."

"Sorry, I don't have anything. And I mean that literally. You made certain I couldn't salvage anything." Laurie was positive that the voice was responsible for the destruction of her home.

"Yes, maybe I did get a tad carried away, but you see I am afraid I let my temper get the better of me. I do try to control it, you understand, but when I am denied what is mine . . ." He let the sentence dangle.

"What do you want?" She was tired of playing games.

"You recently received a package. It is mine."

"Package?" She felt a distinct chill.

"Yes. Do not worry, my dear, I am a reasonable man. You will receive something in the bargain." The smugness was back.

"What could you possibly have that would interest me?"

"Laurie?" Pitsie's voice sounded small and scared, the chill in the room penetrated Laurie and encased her heart.

"Pitsie! Are you hurt? Where are you?" Laurie fired off questions without waiting for answers.

"Help me."

The voice came on the line. "Do not worry, Pitsie is just fine. And we both want her to stay that way." The innuendo hung in the air.

"Either I get a reasonable answer to my questions from Pitsie, or I hang up." It was a bluff, but she had to be sure the voice wasn't using a recording.

The silence on the other end told Laurie what she needed to know.

"Very good, Laurie." Another pause. "I wonder how you knew it was a recording?"

"I watch a lot of television. Anyone who watches *Wiseguy* or *Hunter* knows about recording a kidnap victim. Now, either I talk to Pitsie or I don't talk." Knowing that she might have a slight edge on the kidnapper, gave her some confidence.

"I will contact you within the hour. If your boyfriend returns, I suggest you send him out for pizza." The line went dead.

Laurie allowed herself a moment of sheer unadulterated panic. The towel she had wrapped around her slid to the floor and she crumpled after it. Burying her face in her hands, she cried until her throat ached.

It couldn't have been more than a few minutes before she threw back her shoulders and wiped her eyes. There would be time enough for tears and guilt when Pitsie was safe.

She went to the bathroom and mechanically fixed her hair. She grabbed a pair of jeans and a new sweater, ripping the tags off with sharp, white teeth. A plan was already formulating in the back of her mind. The voice wanted a package that he thought she had. A package that had been sent to her by mistake obviously. Or had it? Hadn't J.D. made some reference to a package. He suspected Pitsie had been receiving packages from Nick. That must be it!

She glanced at her watch and tried to estimate how long J.D. had been gone. She needed to know more about this group Nick was involved with. Nick had to be the one holding Pitsie. He must have taken her from his grandmother's. J.D. probably had a file on the terrorists. Where was he?

The phone began ringing and she made herself let it ring twice. "Yes."

"A trace doesn't work until you pick up the phone. Don't worry I am well aware of these things," the voice said.

"Let me talk to Pitsie."

"Certainly."

A second later Pitsie was on the line. Her voice shook with fear. "Laurie?"

"I'm here, sweetheart. Don't be afraid." That was a really stupid thing to say. Anybody would be afraid.

"I can't help it." The tremor in her voice told Laurie she was on the verge of hysteria.

"I know, sweetie. Don't worry, I'll give Nick what he wants. I'm sure he won't hurt you." Come on Pitsie, tell me what I want to hear.

"I was so wrong, can you forgive me?"

"Oh, Pitsie, there's nothing to forgive." Laurie knew she was on the right track. Pitsie confirmed her suspicions of Nick.

"I'm supposed to answer a question and hang up." Laurie could hear a man issuing orders in the background above the traffic noise.

"Okay, sweetheart. What record were you playing the other day?" Had it only been a few days ago? It seemed like years.

"Van Halen." Pitsie sounded calmer instantly. She hadn't expected Laurie to ask such a mundane question.

She had been agonizing over how to get a secret message to Laurie, but she hadn't needed to. Laurie had already figured out that Nick was involved.

Gaining courage from the fact that Laurie was one step ahead of her kidnappers, Pitsie hung up the phone and faced her captor. Incredibly, only hours before she had envisioned herself married to Nick. Having his children, growing old. Now the only thing she could envision was bashing his head in.

"What did she ask you?" Nick grasped Pitsie's arm much harder than necessary and led her away from his partner.

Pitsie longed for the courage not to answer, but his fingers were gouging into the tender flesh of her upper arm and she knew that he could hurt her. "She just asked what record I was listening to the other day."

"Are you sure that was all? You talked a long time." He led her to the car and refastened the handcuffs she had been wearing since last night.

"I'm sure. She just wanted to tell me everything would be all right." Pitsie's eyes filled with tears as she looked at Nick. "It is gonna be okay, isn't it? I mean you're not gonna hurt me, are you?"

Nick grinned at her and she knew he was enjoying her discomfort. "Now why would I hurt you? As long as your sister does everything she's told, you'll be free by tomorrow night. By the time she figures out how to find you, we'll be long gone. So even if you tell her I was involved, it'll be too late."

Pitsie tried to dampen the flicker of hope deep inside. Laurie already knew Nick was involved. Shoot, she had probably gone to the police—heck, the FBI, as soon as she got off the phone. Once Nick tried to leave the country, he would be arrested. "I won't tell."

"It won't matter. I'll be among friends."

"Friends?"

"Powerful friends. If I thought you wanted to, I'd take you with me."

"Oh Nick, would you?" Pitsie tried to inject some optimism into her voice. Maybe if he thought she was still in love with him, he wouldn't hurt her.

Nick cast a startled glance at Pitsie. "You mean you'd still go with me?"

Pitsie nodded her head vigorously. "I love you! I'd go anywhere you asked. Laurie hates me. She treats me like I'm a baby. You make me feel like I'm a woman."

Nick tapped his fingers on the steering wheel in time to the music blaring from the radio. Pitsie could tell that some part of him believed her. When the other man joined them, Nick quickly maneuvered the car into a service station so the man could place another call to Laurie.

Nick turned to her as the other man left the car. "So you want to go with me?" Hope flared in Pitsie's terrified heart. Not trusting her voice, she nodded and allowed the tears she had been blinking away to trickle down her cheeks. If her drama couch could have seen her, she would have aced his class.

"If you do everything I say, I'll think about it real hard." He reached over and put his lips on hers. She had to bite her tongue to keep from retching. "That's just a sample."

Pitsie realized he had mistaken her shudder of horror for passion. She had read about the male ego in one of Laurie's women's magazines and prayed she could cater to this moron's ego without giving herself away. Her life could depend on it.

Nick quickly whipped through the light traffic to search out another phone booth for his accomplice. Pitsie prayed that Laurie was trying to find her as diligently as they were trying to keep her hidden.

* * *

Laurie was climbing the walls of her hotel room. The man had made two more phone calls leaving instructions for the exchange. So far he had warned her repeatedly about not informing the authorities. He had made reference to the mysterious package once more and then given her a set of instructions to follow.

"Once you have the package, wrap it in Christmas paper. Address the package to Pitsie from Santa. Place it under the tree by Santa's house at the mall. Someone will pick it up. Do not attempt to stop him. He will place a package under the tree with your name on it. Inside will be instructions for finding your sister."

"No."

"No? Ms. Morrison, I hardly think you are in a position to say no."

Clenching her fingers into a fist, she forced herself to continue. "I will leave part of the package with you. Once I have Pitsie, you can have the rest."

"I will get back with you." He hung up and Laurie knew he suspected she was trying to hold him on the line for a trace. There was no way she would have had time to set up a line tap. The voice was running scared. That could either be a blessing or a curse. Laurie hoped if he fell apart he wouldn't take Pitsie with him.

The phone rang only seconds later. "You are more intelligent than I had imagined." The smugness had been replaced by annoyance.

"I'm a big fan of police shows," she said.

"Yes, so you said. However, I do see your point of view."

"Good." Laurie twisted the phone cord tightly around her shaking fingers.

"You will leave half of the money in a package under the tree. I will leave half the instructions. I will arrange for you to drop the rest of the money once you have ascertained your sister's safety."

"How will you manage that?"

"Please do not make the mistake of underestimating me."

"Fine." At least she knew she was looking for a box filled with money.

"Until tomorrow."

Laurie clutched the dead phone for a few brief moments. She punched out J.D.'s number and was rewarded with an irritating message on his machine. "I hate this thing. I need you!"

She slammed down the phone and resumed her pacing. She had to locate this package. It was a safe bet it wasn't in her house, not after all the searches that had been conducted there. It also probably wasn't in the office. Nick claimed to have thoroughly searched both. It must be a fairly small package or it would have been easily found. Come on, Laurie, where would you be if you were a package? Package? Package! If you were a package you would be in the storage room with all the other packages!

Laurie whipped through the room and grabbed her coat and purse. Since her car was still at the mall, she hot-footed it across the Interstate. In her rush she forgot about J.D.

J.D. was madder than a wet hen. It had taken Clifton forever to return his call. When he finally did the connection was so bad J.D. could barely hear him. The man had sworn up and down that he had no knowledge of Laurie's military background. He did know that her parents had been killed five years ago by a terrorist bomb.

"It fits the profile, Westat. Almost everyone in this group has been involved with terrorism at some point. The information we received on her showed that she had ample reason to strike back. We also know she was involved with several high-powered men from the Middle East. Everything we have uncovered points straight at her." Clifton was practically begging J.D. to believe him. Clifton knew he had screwed up on the Morrison case and he also knew J.D. wasn't a forgiving man.

"Clifton, dig your head out of profiles and personality checks for a minute. I need to knew where you received the information on Laurie. Where is the kink? Is someone playing both sides of the fence? Hell, man, we're out here flying blind in a fog! I didn't even want to call you." The implication was clear. Even Clifton was suspect in J.D.'s mind.

"Westat, I swear I don't know what's going on! I have to agree there may be someone we can't trust. For right now, I'd say you were better off solo. This mess has thrown me for a loop. I hate to admit it, but I can't even be sure of the men I've got covering you. So far they haven't done a bang-up job."

J.D.'s jaw muscles ached from clenching them. "You got that right, buddy. I've already had to shake two tails just to get to a phone. If they're yours, call 'em off."

"I don't have anyone on you, just the woman." Clifton sounded petrified.

"Can you be sure?"

Clifton's silence was his answer. J.D. slammed down the phone and headed back to the hotel. He had backtracked for blocks trying to get rid of whoever was tailing him and he had been gone much longer than intended.

As he eased into the parking lot, he noticed one of the cars he had lost earlier. He itched for a confrontation, but the need to get to Laurie was greater.

He noticed a man and woman in the lobby with typical "stake out" expressions on their faces. If they were TAT's, they were sorely in need of further training.

J.D. knocked on the door and tried to peek through

the curtains hiding the interior. A few more knocks and he finally went to the room he had reserved next door. Hopefully Laurie hadn't noticed the connecting door was unlocked.

The knob twisted in his grasp and he stepped into her room. He could smell her perfume and feel the moisture in the room. She must have taken a shower.

"Babe?" He knocked lightly on the partially open bathroom door. Terror slid through him and threatened to choke him. Running a hand over the back of his neck, he held his breath and pushed the door open. He had been prepared to find Laurie lying on the floor in a pool of her own blood. Nothing. His breath hissed from him and he realized his fingers were shaking. Not good. He had to remain in control. Swallowing his emotions he quickly searched the room.

Her towel, slightly damp, lay in an emerald pool beside the bed. A tag for a pair of jeans had been flung to the floor and the box that had contained her new jogging shoes was empty.

He surveyed the bathroom and noted that her toothbrush was dry and her bra hung on the doorknob.

A hurried search of the rest of the boxes told him she had left in a rush. None of her new bras was open and his lady was a little too full-breasted to go braless. He also noted her package of socks was sealed tight.

He started to look for a note but realized that Laurie wasn't aware he could get in. He slammed the door harder than necessary in his haste to get to the front desk. Both the man and woman in the lobby stared blatantly at him as he strode to the desk.

"Did Laurie Morrison leave a message for me? J.D. Westat." At this point he didn't care if half the operatives in the country heard.

"I have no messages from Ms. Morrison."

J.D. walked to the payphone and dialed the numbers

required to play back the messages on his answering machine. His heart plummeted when he heard her. The panic tinging her voice said more than the words ever could have. She was scared and in trouble. He had been playing "lose the agent" and she needed him.

Running on a lethal combination of terror and anger, he stalked to his Bronco and with a rather earthy gesture to the man in the plain, brown car, he sped off. He didn't have time for games.

The brown car pulled onto the snow-covered street just moments after J.D. With a sick grin, J.D. pressed down on the gas and said a quick "thank you" for four-wheel drive. A glance in the rearview mirror confirmed the brown car couldn't hope to keep up with him.

J.D.'s apartment was cold and unfortunately empty. He had hoped Laurie might try to find him here. He went to his bedroom and rapidly twisted the dials on the combination lock securing an inner compartment in the back of his closet.

He had spent several hours installing surveillance equipment in the mall's storage room last night. A blinking red light informed him that someone had been in the room. The cameras were set on a motion activator. He rewound the back-up tape and watched the miniature television monitor.

For a few seconds he wondered if the equipment was malfunctioning. All he saw was an empty room. He pressed the fast-forward button and just as he was about to flip the off switch, he saw her.

Laurie walked into the storage room and began searching through the small stack of packages. He felt the bile rise up in his throat.

She was systematically searching through the smaller boxes. She was carelessly tossing the packages around, much the same as he had only yesterday. His eyes burned into the monitor as he watched her pick up the package from Davidson. She clutched it to her chest, the look on her face pure joy.

The little witch! She had fooled him every way there was to fool a man. She had bested him at his job and stolen his heart. What chance did a mere mortal man have against a siren like her?

He reached up and flicked off the equipment. Not bothering to fasten the locks or secure the equipment, he left.

He knew what had to be done but he couldn't seem to shift out of slow-motion. Every footstep took an eternity. The cold wind stung his eyes, made them water. Or at least he convinced himself it was the cold that brought tears to his eyes.

TWELVE

J.D. stood before her door, debating on the proper course of action. Should he reason with her? Threaten her? Offer to run away with her? Stop it, Westat! That line of thinking is suicidal. He gathered his courage and knocked on the door.

Laurie opened the door and flung herself into his arms. "Where have you been? I've been calling all over for you."

J.D. fought the urge to wrap her in his arms. "Yeah, I got the message."

Laurie eased herself from J.D. and tried to read the emotions running across his face. "What's wrong?"

"What's wrong?" he whispered.

"What's wrong!" he roared. "I'll tell you what's wrong. You! I can't believe I was so stupid. You just looked at me with those big green eyes and I believed . . . I stood up for you, I . . . , I . . ." J.D. couldn't find the words for his anger and betrayal.

"I have no idea what you're talking about. Or should I say raving about." Laurie stepped back from him. "If you'll calm down a minute, maybe we can figure this out."

"Oh, I've got you figured out, lady. But good! You bat those gorgeous eyes at some unsuspecting male and he flips. Well, I flipped all right, but you can bet it's a mistake I won't make again." He paused to catch his breath after his tirade. "Now I'm sure you know what I'm here for, so why don't you just assume the position and we'll get this over with." He eased a pair of sparkling silver handcuffs from the back pocket of his jeans.

"Have you lost your mind?!"

J.D. growled and made a grab for her wrist. Before he had hold of her, she slipped from him and flew across the bed. He stormed after her and she deftly eluded him. "J.D., stop it! This isn't funny."

"It wasn't meant to be. Now hold still, don't make this any harder than it has to be."

"I'm sure not going to make it easy." Laurie frantically tried to reason J.D.'s actions through her mind. There was only one reason she could think of to explain his actions.

He reached for her again and she clasped his wrist and twisted her body alongside his. Leveling herself at his much bigger body, she slid her leg between his and in a series of twists and turns, J.D. found himself flat on his back.

Laurie took advantage of his momentary surprise to grab the handcuffs and lock them around his wrist. After passing the chain under the dresser, she secured his other wrist.

The look on his face was almost funny. Laurie quickly ripped the television cable from the wall and wrapped it around his thrashing legs. Finally, she reached into the stack of boxes containing her new purchases and grabbed something to shove in his mouth.

Laurie was panting with her efforts as she straddled

J.D.'s now subdued body. "Now . . . are you . . . going to listen . . . or not?"

J.D. grunted slightly and she looked at him. His eyes had softened but his face was the most amazing shade of red. She knew he was furious, but right now she didn't have the time to deal with fragile male egos. "Uncle?"

J.D. bucked at his restraints and continued to make ugly sounds, despite his gag. Reaching over, Laurie pinched his nostrils until he struggled for air. "Now, hush."

J.D. knew she could easily withhold his air until he passed out if he wasn't careful. As much as it galled him, she had him thoroughly hog-tied.

Laurie rose to her feet and placed one foot across J.D.'s throat slightly constricting his air. "You are aware of what can happen if I press down?" She didn't try to hide the anger in her voice.

J.D. grumbled his understanding. Oh, she was a pro—no doubt. Even if he managed to throw her off-balance, he still risked a crushed windpipe.

"Now that we understand each other." Laurie grasped the edge of the nailed-down dresser to prevent losing her balance, thus causing any accidents. "Where is she?"

J.D.'s brows knitted together in confusion. He shook his head to indicate he didn't know what she was talking about. Immediately her foot applied more pressure. His tongue pushed against the silky cloth in his mouth.

She removed her foot and knelt down beside him. "If I remove the gag, will you behave yourself?"

J.D. nodded, he had a few questions he wanted to ask, too.

Laurie reached for his gag and noticed it was her new black nightie. Biting the inside of her cheek against the laughter welling up inside her, she pulled the material from his lips.

J.D.'s eyes held hers for a brief, intimate moment before the shutters came back down.

"You answer my questions first." Her voice brooked no argument. J.D. nodded, not yet trusting his control.

"Where is Pitsie?"

"I don't have any idea."

Laurie eyed him carefully, assessing his honesty. "Okay. Are you working with Davidson?"

J.D.'s dark eyebrows shot up. "What's the matter, sweetheart, afraid lover-boy is on the double take?"

Laurie wadded her gown into a ball. "I said answer my questions, not make sarcastic remarks."

J.D. shrugged as best he could with his arms locked over his head. "No, I have no contact with Davidson."

"Are you both involved with the same people?"

"No."

Laurie noticed his eyes never flickered, nor did his pupils dilate. His breathing was even. All of his body language screamed he was telling the truth. Of course, he was a trained agent. It was possible he could control his body and still be lying. "Do you know who took my sister?"

"What?" J.D.'s startled cry was quickly followed by a string of obscenities when he banged his head on the corner of the dresser. "You mean she's missing?"

"J.D., if you didn't come to kidnap me, what did you come here for?" Tenderness edged her words.

"I came here to arrest you on a whole slew of charges, the biggest being international terrorism."

Laurie slid back against the bed, her mouth hanging open. "Me? I thought we had that settled."

"So did I," he said, looking pointedly at the iron encircling his wrists.

Logic warred with emotion. "What changed your mind?"

J.D. held his own private battle. "I set up surveillance in the storage room. You were on the tapes."

"Pretty incriminating," Laurie agreed. It was all so logical. "Why didn't you tell me about the peeper?"

J.D. had the decency to look sheepish. "After all the excitement last night, I forgot. I mean last night was pretty, uh . . . illuminating."

Laurie nibbled on her lower lip, obviously debating the best course of action. "I think a little further illumination is called for. The skeletons in our closets go pretty deep."

Laurie asked for the keys to the cuffs and held her breath as she slid her fingers into his front pocket. The material was so tight it scraped the top of her knuckles as she extricated the tiny keys.

J.D. barely allowed her enough time to unlock one cuff before he sat up and took the key from her. His face was a study in warring emotions.

His square jaw jutted with barely concealed anger and his normally full lips were drawn into a grim line. He kept his eyes averted, but Laurie caught a glimpse of compassion in their blue depths. As angry and embarrassed as he was, he was still concerned for her.

J.D. untied the cable around his legs and stood. He glowered at her for a second before hauling her to her feet. "You're right. It's time we got it all out in the open. No secrets, no half-truths."

"Will you help me find Pitsie?" She held her breath. If he wouldn't, the odds against her were much greater.

"Stupid question, Morrison." The harsh words were spoken with an abundance of love and tenderness. Laurie felt her heart swell.

"Thank you. I understand we're both trusting our 'little voices' right now," she said.

"Has anyone contacted you?" He was all business.

"Yes. I think it was Davidson, but he was disguising his voice. There are at least two of them." She went on to explain what had transpired while he was gone. By the time she had finished she was angry all over again. "So you see, I had to find that stupid package and get the money from it."

"I understand, babe." He reached out and ran a finger down her cheek. It was the first time they had touched except in anger. She flew into his arms and this time he wrapped her tightly to him. "That means we've got until tomorrow to formulate our plan."

"Then you believe me, about not being involved with him?"

J.D. heard the underlying harshness in her voice and knew she was fighting tears. "Laurie, I want to believe you more than I've ever wanted anything in my life."

"J.D., I can't prove that I'm not involved with him." Laurie blinked against the pain. "I'm not even sure what he's involved in, but you've got to have some kind of gut instinct. You know, your little voice. What does it tell you?"

J.D. stopped pacing and flopped down on the bed, throwing his forearm over his eyes. "Yeah. I just don't know if my instincts are all that reliable these days."

"Why not?"

He reached out his hand and she grasped it. "Because I've never been in love with a suspect before. There's a hard and fast rule—Do not, under any circumstances, become emotionally involved in a case."

"I've heard that one. I can see where it makes good sense."

J.D. rolled to his side and propped himself up on one elbow. "I lost my objectivity before and people died because of it. I've lost it now." J.D. hated the memories burning their way from the past.

"Do you need to tell me what happened?" J.D. couldn't help notice she had asked if he "needed" to tell her, not that she "wanted" to know.

"No secrets, remember." He didn't want to tell her, but she needed to know. "Get comfortable. It's not a pleasant story."

Laurie scooted to the top of the bed and sat back against the pillows. She turned her face to him, willing to listen.

"Ten years ago I began working the Middle East. I was so full of myself I should have had two social security numbers. I had just come out of Eastern Europe with a string of successes under my belt and I was gonna clean up Lebanon over night."

Laurie could hear the disgust in his voice at the man he had been. She longed to tell him it didn't matter, but she was afraid it might.

"I infiltrated several terrorist factions with an ease that should have surprised me. I took it upon myself to decide which group posed the biggest threat. My superiors tried to steer me toward a religious faction in Tripoli, but I decided that my talents should be put to much better use. I went after the man himself." He uttered a harsh chuckle. "If I could get in with Jamal Ahadnah, I would be on the inside track." J.D. was so caught up in his memories, he didn't notice that Laurie had gone deathly still.

"I went to all the right places, met all the right people, did all the right things. I spent five years ingratiating myself with Ahadnah's people. Everyone believed my hard-luck story. Poor American, sent to Viet Nam, deserted, without family or country. I was better than just alone, I was a man ready to strike back at a country that had destroyed my young life." J.D. snorted and began pacing at the foot of the bed.

"What happened?" She had to know.

"Oh, I became indispensable to Jamal. He asked my advice on everything. When he traveled to America, I told him where to stay, what to eat, who to be seen with. Of course, since he always took my advice, he was much easier to keep track of in the States. Clifton was always updated before every trip. Since I was a deserter, I never traveled with Jamal." He stopped for a minute and looked at Laurie, not really seeing her.

"One time Jamal returned talking about this beautiful blonde American woman who had captured his heart. She was very young, I don't think she was even out of college, but I couldn't be bothered with her. Jamal would rattle on and on about her, but I would just tune him out. I had spent five years becoming his confidant. I wanted to hear about terrorist attacks, not blonde bombshells.

"I was in such a hurry to bring him down. I longed for him to reveal his 'grand scheme' to me. I didn't have the time to worry about what his sick, twisted mind had in store for some cheerleader."

J.D. stopped for a minute and buried his face in his hands. He seemed to be debating whether to continue. Laurie reached out and touched him, willing him to go on.

"Finally, almost too late, I realized what he had planned. He wanted me to help him kidnap the girl and bring her to him. You have to understand, he was the kind of man who could easily take the girl and no one would ever have a clue."

"I know," Laurie whispered, but he didn't hear her.

"I refused. I couldn't believe he wouldn't forget her, but he persisted. Finally, once he decided I wouldn't help him, he sought help elsewhere. He managed to convince the girl to fly in for a visit. Simple kidnapping, the victim came willingly across half the globe. Poor girl, she must have been incredibly innocent.

Women are no more than chattel in that part of the world. Once she was within his compound, she was his and no questions asked."

"No questions asked." J.D. noticed the hollow ring in Laurie's words and looked at her for the first time since he had started his tirade. "Are you sure you want to hear this?"

"No, but go ahead." Laurie pulled her knees up to her chest and wrapped her arms around them.

"Well, once I found out she was in the compound I tried to devise a plan of escape for her. Jamal was furious that her parents had the nerve to demand the government take formal action. He tried to get the girl to marry him, but she refused. He literally threw her in the dungeon. I searched for her everywhere. I had a new obsession. The funny thing is I never even met her. I had only seen her from a distance, but she looked so sweet and pure and well, hell, I don't know. I just couldn't stand the thought of Jamal using her like his other women. So I forgot about my plan to save the world. I managed to make contact with the girl through a slave. We passed notes for a few weeks. That in itself was one of the most ignorant things I've ever done. If Jamal had found out, we would have been barbecued." He stopped for a minute and walked to the sink and began unwrapping a plastic cup. After chugging two glasses of water, he continued.

"Those notes were the high point of my days. Even locked up and scared to death, she was fabulous. Sometimes her notes were so full of joy and life, so funny. Well, enough of that." He resumed his pacing. "I lost my objectivity and I killed people in the process. I threatened Clifton. Finally, in all my arrogance, I decided that the only way to secure her release was to kill Jamal." He shook his head. "It was so easy."

"J.D., stop!"

He didn't hear her. "I went to his room and we sat around drinking and plotting. He was in a great mood. He told me he finally had the leverage he needed to force the girl to marry him. Her parents had flown over to try and arrange her release and he was going to kidnap them, too. He began to gloat about how the girl would grovel for her parents lives and then when she had bound herself to him, he would execute the people anyway. He felt he had to set an example." J.D.'s eyes and voice had grown chillingly calm. "I let him ramble on about his plans for the girl. No big deal, I knew he would be dead in a matter of hours. I had slipped several doses of a very powerful poison into his drinks. It was too easy. I watched his face turn purple, his eyes bug out and I felt absolutely nothing. The man lay on the floor at my feet, begging for his life, and I just sat there and watched until he was dead. I calmly washed his glass and put it away, then poured a small amount of wine into another glass and wrapped his dead fingers around it. I didn't know how much of an investigation his people would fool with, but I didn't want them to trace it to me until I had the girl out of the country. I put him to bed and left. A few hours later the entire compound was a madhouse. People were screaming and throwing themselves on the ground in grief. The man was the devil incarnate, but his people adored him."

"What happened to the girl?"

J.D. chuckled a hard mirthless laugh. "Well, I figured that my plan was foolproof. I didn't count on the fool being me. I waltzed to the prison area. The guard told me she had been executed for the death of Jamal. Apparently, he had left orders for the girl to be sent to him after I left. When she got there he was already dead. I guess it took her a while before she approached the bed and discovered him. She probably screamed and the guard ran in. He assumed she had killed his beloved master and slit her throat."

"What did you do?"

"Honey, I was out of there so fast it would've made your head swim. I had blown five years of work and hadn't even been able to save one scared, innocent, little girl. I might as well have put a gun to her head myself." His voice was rife with self-loathing. "There was a time when I considered putting one to my own."

"But you couldn't have known!" She got to her knees and reached for him. He ignored her.

"Clifton tried to assure me that I wasn't responsible. I mean, it was just a series of unfortunate accidents. I tried to go see her parents afterward, but I was a coward." J.D. ran a hand over his face and was surprised to find his cheeks wet. "Anyway, I had had enough. I came back to the States and just drifted for a while. When I got the word that Granny was sick I came back here. I still have nightmares about what Jamal must have done to that girl."

"It was more horrible than you can imagine." Her voice was barely audible.

"What?" For the first time he turned his attention to Laurie.

She looked at him for one soul-searching moment and got off the bed to find her purse. She shuffled through her wallet for a minute and extracted a worn piece of paper. "Here."

J.D. took the paper from her and read the words. "Where the hell did you get this!" He grabbed her wrist so tightly she thought he might snap it in two.

"It's mine." Her voice held none of her pain.

"That's a lie. Where did you get this? No lies." He towered over her.

"It's mine, J.D. You wrote it to me five years ago.

It's the only one I dared keep." Her voice was unwavering, her eyes steady.

He pushed her from him with such force she fell against the table. "How?"

"J.D., I was that blonde American cheerleader."

He looked in her eyes and knew it to be true. He opened his mouth but there were no words for the turmoil in his head.

"Can you hold me?" She stood quietly by him, needing his strength. He held his arms open and she went to him. They clung together for a few minutes before she explained her outrageous claim.

"I was very good at attracting the Middle Eastern types. You know how they love blondes."

J.D. nodded and kissed the top of her coppery head.

"Well, I bleached my hair, stuffed myself into two inches worth of dress and set out to capture me a bad guy." She closed her eyes tightly. "My bad guy was Jamal Ahadnad. Some coincidence, huh?"

"Yeah."

"Well, my superiors couldn't believe their luck when he asked me to fly over. They had been trying to get a man on the inside for a while and I was their ace. I was to send out vital information about the compound itself, Jamal's man-power, any pillow talk."

J.D. growled but didn't interrupt.

"No, there was no pillow talk. A man like Jamal wouldn't take a woman to his bed and then talk to her." An involuntary shiver ran through her. "Things ran pretty smooth for a while, then Jamal started talking marriage. I tried to bluff my way out but he finally threw me in that hell-hole. Then one day, I got a note. It wasn't much of one, all it said was 'you've got a friend.' Made me think of the James Taylor song. I sang that song over and over just to keep my sanity. I waited for each note with more longing than my next breath."

"Why did you save this one?" J.D. held up the torn paper.

"It was the one that told me you loved me," she said simply, amazed he didn't understand.

"What are you talkin' about, all it says is, 'we're outta here.'"

"Yeah. All the other notes talked about getting me out, nothing about my secret admirer. That was the only time you mentioned both of us going."

J.D. understood. She had suspected her friend was one of Jamal's men. For a man like that to leave everything for a woman, it would have been love. "But now that you know it was me and not one of his men?"

"It means that you loved me even more. You were willing to give up all that you had worked for." She cast him a sly glance. "You still are."

"You bet."

"Anyway, I hadn't been summoned to Jamal's chambers for over a month. For that I was eternally grateful. The man was a pig."

"Did he hurt you?" The question was quiet.

"I don't think you want to know."

"Yeah, I do."

"Yes, he hurt me. A lot and often. He hurt me mentally and physically. He hurt me in ways I didn't know I could be hurt. He stole my freedom and he killed my parents. He forced himself on me and couldn't understand my revulsion. And he killed the man I loved." She hugged J.D. tightly. "At least I thought he killed the man I loved."

"He raped you?"

"J.D., you know what kind of man he was. What kind of women he was used to. He didn't think of it as rape, he felt he was bestowing a great honor on me. He even offered to marry me when he discovered I was a virgin . . ."

"A virgin! My Lord, Laurie, I am so sorry." He held her so tightly she couldn't breath.

"It wasn't your fault. I went there willingly. J.D., in this business losing your virginity isn't really that big a deal. My superiors were sorry, they hated that the man had raped me. They made me go for counseling as soon as I got back. But let's face it, when you deal with massive death counts, rape comes in way down on the list of priorities."

"You don't sound upset."

"That's because I've had five years to come to terms with it. You've only had five minutes. I still have problems with intimacy, but I've noticed an improvement in that area lately." She smiled up at him and he kissed her gently.

"Do you still see a shrink?"

"A psychologist. She has become a very good friend. She's helped me see that what I went through doesn't have to scar me for the rest of my life. I don't have to give Jamal that kind of power."

"Sounds like a smart lady."

"She is. You'll like her."

"What happened the night of Jamal's death?" There were still a dozen unanswered questions.

"I'm not sure now. I was sitting there among the bugs when I was summoned. I was told Jamal would expect me after his friend had left. I was bathed, plucked, powdered, and painted. I was left naked and covered with a heavy cloak and veil. Then I waited."

"Until I was gone."

"I suppose. Anyway, I entered his bedchamber for what I had determined was the last time. I had managed to hide the knife I had used at dinner. Sort of a silly plan, but I knew I couldn't let my friend risk his life. And I couldn't wait around for help from the outside."

"You had decided to kill him?" J.D. shook his head at her plan.

"Yes. When I entered the bedchamber it was dark, but that wasn't any surprise. Jamal was into all sorts of weird games."

"That I don't want to know."

"I didn't think you did. When my eyes adjusted to the light, I saw him in the bed. I thought he was asleep, so I merely walked over and plunged the knife into his heart. He never made a sound. I jerked the brocade curtain down and used it to jump out the window. By the time my feet hit the ground everything broke loose."

"How were you discovered so fast?"

"Apparently, Jamal had decided that three wasn't a crowd and the other girl arrived just after I killed him."

"Then that was the girl that was executed."

"Yes, at least I guess so. I was concentrating on making my way out of there. I didn't stop to listen to gossip."

"What about your parents?" He hated asking, but needed to.

"They should never have been involved. I didn't even know they were until it was too late. Jamal was right, I would have promised him anything. Anyhow, a photographer took a picture of me on Jamal's yacht and sold it to one of the tabloids. Luckily, I had changed my appearance enough that I was barely recognizable. But dear old Dad saw his little darling hob-nobbing with a known terrorist and decided to make waves. Since my parents were unaware of my extended career, Dad stirred things up. If I had known, I could have let him know. Before my boss knew what was going on, my parents were headed for Jamal's compound trying to catch up with me. It didn't take much really, just a tiny little bomb and they got the message." Her voice was leaden.

"Oh, baby." He rocked back and forth holding her against him.

"For years I've blamed myself. If I hadn't been involved in the first place, or if I had at least confided in my dad, they would be alive today."

"You can't know that. It wasn't your fault. I can see how you would blame yourself. It's easier than trying to accept that we really have no control over some things."

"My psychologist says that I'm conceited. She's always asking me what new world crisis I'm responsible for today. I'm still not over the guilt, and I have a heck of a time with relationships, but I'm getting there." She threw him a tremulous smile and felt the ice melt from her heart.

He knew they both had old scars that might be with them the rest of their lives. He also knew this woman would understand his dark moods. "Yeah, I guess we both are."

Laurie slipped her fingers between his and squeezed. "I trust you, J.D. Not only with my life, but with my sister's."

"Thank you." He kissed her for a long time and when he finally let her go, he felt ready to tackle the world. "We better get started. Santa Claus is coming to town."

THIRTEEN

Friday morning was a pink and gold spectacle that should have lightened Laurie's heart. She never noticed how the gentle morning sun glinted off the icicles from the melting snow. The streets had been cleared and traffic was back to normal. She dressed in the first thing she picked up and waited for J.D. to knock on the connecting door.

She had surprised him by being happy about the adjoining rooms. She had even debated on asking him to stay with her, but she knew they were in no shape to deal with their emotions.

J.D. had held her until she fell asleep and then he had slipped into his room. He forced his mind to relax using an old technique he had learned years ago. He needed to be ready for whatever Davidson had in store for them tomorrow.

Laurie had tiptoed into his room just before dawn and watched him sleep. A light feathery kiss had startled him awake and he pulled her down next to him before she could scurry away. By the time he let her go, her robe had ridden up her thighs and the sheet revealed that J.D. did indeed wear his underwear to bed.

"Ready, babe?" J.D. poked his still damp head through the door.

"As I'll ever be." She looked lost but determined. J.D. assured her that she was gorgeous in her bright green knit dress and red and green pumps. He wanted to assure her that nothing would go wrong, but he knew how easily that could become a lie.

He followed her to the mall and parked next to her. He had to assume he was being watched, so he made sure he was highly visible. He kissed her good-bye and then drove away.

Laurie's office still held a faint hint of the gas so she decided to avoid it if at all possible. The memories were abruptly painful. Instead, she spent the first hour walking through the mall, chatting with the merchants and walkers. It could have been any Friday. It should have been any Friday. Pitsie shouldn't be tied up scared to death and Laurie shouldn't have been thrust back into a life she had struggled to obliterate. She noticed Henry looking about as down as she felt. "Where's Margaret?"

"I don't know." Henry's answer was abrupt, almost rude, and his usually pleasant face was drawn into a scowl.

"Guess I can take a hint." She turned to leave.

"I'm sorry, honey."

She glanced back at him and realized she wasn't the only one with problems this bright winter day. "Did you have a fight?"

"I don't think so." He shook his head. "Wednesday everything was hunky-dory. Then all of a sudden she started acting like I had the plague. Just when I thought everything was workin' like a charm . . ." Henry broke off as if he had said too much.

"Henry, you don't have to explain anything to me." Laurie placed her hand on his shoulder.

"I guess I better not air my dirty laundry."

"I'm here if you need me." She patted his shoulder and wondered at the change in Henry. A week ago he had kept her from her work at every opportunity, telling her stories of his stint in the Navy, his grandchildren, and a dozen other topics. He would demand she tell him everything that was happening in her life, as well as Pitsie's and Bubba's. She had noticed the change, but her mind was so occupied that Henry's problems would have to wait.

Her mind automatically filed away the people she met on her trek through the mall. Old friends had taken on sinister qualities, strangers seemed to be lurking around every corner.

"Stop it!" she said aloud. She was getting paranoid and if she didn't control herself, she wouldn't be of any help to Pitsie or J.D.

J.D. had managed to formulate a fairly decent plan, but she would have felt better if they could have called in some help with its execution. Execution! Her mind was certainly running on a morbid track. All morning she had thought in terms of mourning and death and pain. Her knuckles were white as she clenched her fists against the thoughts. Why had Bubba brought Nick Davidson home in the first place? Why had he stayed at their home if his grandmother lived in town? Why had . . . Grandmother! She had completely forgotten the grandmother. In all the time she and J.D. had gone over and over every aspect of the situation she had neglected to tell him about Nick's grandmother. She spun on her heel and flew across the mall to her office.

"I'll be on the phone," she told Carrie and whisked her pink messages off the desk. Carrie, already on the phone, merely raised a hand.

She shut her door quietly, careful not to betray her sense of urgency. She didn't want to alarm her co-workers. Frankie was such a macho sweetie he would insist on becoming involved. She flipped through the morning's messages but there was nothing from Nick or J.D. She ruffled through her drawers looking for Nick's grandmother's phone number. Where had she put it?

"Finally." She sighed and quickly punched out the numbers. She caught her breath when someone actually answered the phone.

"Is someone there?"

"Yes, this is Laurie Morrison, could I speak to Pitsie?"

"Oh, Laurie, I'm sorry, she isn't here. Didn't she come home last night?"

Crud, of course Nick had probably told his grandmother he was taking Pitsie home. "No, she didn't. I haven't seen her and I'm getting worried." That was an understatement.

"I'm sure she's fine. Nick was going to drop her off on his way to the airport."

"Nick was here?" Laurie prayed the old lady might not be aware that she could be setting her own grandson up.

"Yes, it was such a surprise. We were getting ready for bed and he waltzed through the door. I was so happy to see him. You know, I've been against him and Pitsie seeing each other, but when I saw the way they looked at each other. Oh, Laurie dear, you don't suppose they've eloped do you?" The grandmother sounded shocked.

"No, I don't think they eloped. Besides, Nick is stationed in Cuba and I don't think they allow spouses over there." She didn't want to worry the old woman.

"Do you think she's okay?"

"I'm sure she is. I just realized I don't even know your name or address." Man, she must be losing her mind.

"That's fine, dear. Good-bye." The phone went dead.

Laurie still didn't know her name or address. She

crossed to the large bookshelf lining one wall of her office and pulled down the city cross directory. Unless the phone number was unlisted, it would be in here along with the name and address.

The blasted number was unlisted. She would have to use a few old techniques to get the number from the phone company. She tossed the book in the general direction of the wall and it bounced off the door.

"What happened?" Carrie immediately poked her head in the door.

"Frustration!"

"Frustration? I figured that new security guard would have taken care of that little problem by now. Or is that the reason for your frustration?" Laurie enjoyed Carrie's warm-hearted teasing.

"No, he hasn't taken care of 'that little problem' and that is probably part of what has me frustrated. Along with the fact that someone has vandalized my happy existence."

Carrie was instantly sober. "I forgot. I'm sorry."

"Don't be. I was having a pity party for one and you just reminded me they're no fun."

"Laurie, you know if there is anything I can do . . . maybe give J.D. a hint?"

"He doesn't need any hints, believe me. It isn't for lack of trying that things haven't worked out."

"Ooooh, sounds interesting. Want to talk about it?" Carrie wiggled her eyebrows.

"No, and get your mind out of the gutter. One of us down there is enough for the office."

Carrie giggled and closed the door. Laurie was feeling far from her usual flippant self, but she couldn't let Carrie know. If Carrie suspected something was really wrong, she would bring in the big guns and Laurie wasn't sure she could maintain the facade around Frankie.

He had a way of getting past her barricades and worming the truth out of her.

She glanced at her watch. Thirty more minutes until Santa arrived. Carrie had seen to the photographer and Laurie knew the children were already lining up in front of the ice house in center court.

Santa would arrive in a helicopter and sit on a huge red velvet throne. His sack would be loaded down with candy canes to give to the little ones who sat on his lap and told him their deepest wishes. He would be stuffed with batting and have a fake white beard. This particular Santa would have a little something else tucked under his red velvet coat. This Santa would be packing a .38.

"You are going to do what?" she had asked last night.

"I'm gonna be Santa. You know, Good Ole Saint Nick."

"I guess I'm stupid, but why?"

"I figure Davidson better not see hide nor hair of me." He waited for her agreement. "So if I'm padded and covered with a glob of white hair, he won't. I'll tell the Santa you've already hired to show up a little late. I'll say I want to surprise you. Davidson said you were to sit on Santa's lap and there would be a package under the tree, right?"

"Yes." Laurie was beginning to see a method to his madness.

"So you sit on my lap and I'll be able to protect you. After the exchange is made, I'll take a break and the real Santa can take over."

The plan seemed to be the simplest and most logical one they had hatched all night, so Laurie agreed. She was truly grateful he had devised a plan that would enable him to stick close to her.

She made her way to Santa's house and began assuring restless toddlers that, yes, Santa was on his way.

She glanced at the adults gathered around and noticed that Margaret and Henry had made up. They were standing next to the huge tree watching the children.

Several new packages had been placed under the tree and she longed to examine them. Most of the presents were donations for the needy that would be gathered up at the end of each day. She forced herself to stay away from the tree and those packages.

Since Nick wasn't working alone, she knew his partner must already be at the mall. Watching her. She eyed those around her. Henry waved gaily and for once Margaret seemed happy to see her.

"Where is your young man?" she asked in her odd accent.

"I'm not sure. He had some errands to run this morning." She decided to try to be nice to the woman. "He said he probably wouldn't be through until late this afternoon."

Remarkably this cheered Margaret even more. "Then you must have lunch with us. We won't take no for an answer."

Laurie glanced at Henry and noticed he was as puzzled by Margaret's change of heart as she was. "I'll have to let you know. We're pretty busy today."

"Of course, we understand. If you get too busy, just give me a holler. I'll be glad to help anyway I can." Henry slipped his arm around Laurie and gave her a quick hug.

Laurie suddenly found herself wishing she could tell him everything. She knew she couldn't involve him, but it would feel so good to have someone else know.

The whap-whap of the helicopter blades permeated the air and the children began to dance around. Laurie had always loved this day. She liked knowing she helped put smiles on those faces.

"HO HO HO!" J.D. was striding through the glass doors and waving. The children squealed and waved back. One little boy was so excited he wet his pants. His embarrassed mother led him away and Laurie felt sorry for him.

She had warned J.D. that Santa usually had to endure one or two accidents. Along with scared and crying babies that mothers would perch on his lap for a picture. Laurie had never been able to understand why anyone would want a picture of their child screaming on Santa's lap, but every year there were a few that were determined to instill the Christmas spirit in their little darlings, or else.

J.D. never even glanced her way, but she knew they were equally aware of each other. It didn't seem to matter that they were in a powder keg situation; she felt her temperature rise every time she was within fifty feet of him.

J.D. had his picture taken with about twenty children when the newspaper arrived for photos.

"We thought you might like a picture of me on Santa's lap, Mike," she offered the reporter.

"Sure, great. I mean Santa's for the big people with bucks, right?"

"Don't be such a cynic, Mike." Laurie placed a hand over her stomach to squelch the tremors. She had prayed for this moment, but now that it was here, she was terrified. What if she opened the box and it was a pipe bomb? All those little children would be hurt. What if she opened it and found Pitsie's ear? She held out her hand to J.D. and climbed on his lap.

"Well, now, isn't this a treat for Santa." A few people standing around chuckled. Laurie felt the blood rush to her frozen fingers at his touch and he squeezed her for reassurance.

She sat on his knee, being careful not to put her entire weight on it. She may have been scared to death and involved in an international crime, but she was still a woman. A woman who didn't want her man to realize just how heavy she was. J.D. pressed down on her and she was forced to sit fully on his lap.

"Come on, Laurie, babe, that's a grimace not a smile." Mike peered over his camera.

"Sorry." She plastered her best fake smile on and waited for the flash. Temporarily blinded she asked, "Okay, Santa, where is my present?"

"As soon as I get rid of these spots I'll find it. But first, have you been a good girl?" His hand was massaging the small of her back where no one could see. He could feel the tension radiating from her.

Frankie squinted at the packages and found the one with her name on it. "Here ya go."

Not trusting herself to open the package with dignity, she decided to open it in her office. "Thank you, Santa, I'll put it under my tree until Christmas."

J.D.'s eyes questioned her but he didn't argue. He was about to say that Santa needed a break when he noticed Henry poking among the presents. A quick glance at Laurie and he was off the throne and flying at the old man.

Henry landed among the presents with a thud and J.D. quickly secured the elderly man. Henry had turned red in the face from the exertion and Laurie's mouth hung open. J.D. plucked the package from Henry's fingers and gave it to Laurie. "Is this the one you put under the tree?"

"No! This has Margaret's name on it." Laurie reached over and pulled J.D. off Henry. Frankie didn't know what was going on but he was doing his best to calm the crowd. Laurie heard him mention Santa protecting the presents, but that was a minor problem at the moment. J.D. began helping Henry to his feet.

"I know you don't understand, but I did have a reason for acting like a fool. I'm sorry." J.D. helped Henry straighten himself.

"I'll explain later, Henry." Laurie handed him the box with the jeweler's seal on the corner.

"If this has anything to do with Davidson or TAT you had better explain now. Later may be too late." Henry succeeded in dropping both their jaws.

"Let's go to your office," J.D. mumbled under his breath and led her by the elbow.

"What do you think is going on?" she whispered.

"Your guess is as good as mine," he answered.

Carrie was helping the real Santa into his suit when they got to the office and she looked up questioningly. "Don't ask," Laurie said.

J.D. cut off any further conversation by half dragging her into her office and closing the door behind them. "What do you have to do with TAT?"

Henry cleared his throat and sat down in one of the chairs opposite Laurie's desk. He would not be intimidated. "I work for the government. I've been keeping my eye on both of you."

Laurie lowered herself into the other chair and put her head in her hands. "Call the boys in the white coats, I've lost my mind."

J.D. felt pretty much the same way, but he wouldn't let it show. "Which government do you work for?"

Henry lifted an eyebrow as if to tell J.D. that such a question was ridiculous. "Suffice it to say, I'm well acquainted with both of your superiors. That isn't the problem at the moment."

"No, the problem is they have my sister." Laurie didn't appreciate being forgotten.

"Patsy?" Henry shot out of his chair. "Has anyone been notified about this? Are you trying to get yourself killed? And the child?" He looked like he was about to continue when J.D. cut him off.

"I don't plan on any killing, except for Davidson."

Laurie managed to clear her mind and concentrate on what was being said. "How did you know my sister's name is really Patsy?"

Henry stopped arguing with J.D. and sat down by her again. "I've known your family for many years. I knew your dad when he was in the service. That was one reason I wanted to be on your assignment."

"Just how many branches of the government are assigned to me?" Laurie was incredulous.

"That I don't know." Henry cleared his throat. "As a matter of fact, I'm doing a little free-lance right now."

"Why?" This from J.D.

"Something's not right. Not with either one of you. I've known about you for years, boy. Heard all about your great times with TAT. Although how you can stand working for Clifton, I'll never know."

"At least we're in agreement there." J.D. felt himself warming toward the elderly man.

"Someone began poking into your records a few months ago, I had your file flagged so I was notified. I couldn't determine who had been playing with your file for several weeks. Then a buddy of mine came up with TAT. Sure enough, J.D. showed up. It just took me a while to determine whether or not he was a good guy."

"What have you decided?" J.D. grinned.

"I don't think you're planning to kill her, but the verdict is still out." J.D. read the message behind the words loud and clear. He had better not hurt her either.

J.D. sat quietly on the edge of the desk, one denim-clad leg swinging over the side. "Better open that package now."

Laurie glanced at the box in her hand. "You don't think it's wired do you?"

Henry shook his head, but Laurie still looked to J.D. for confirmation. "I doubt it; you've still got something he wants."

Laurie nodded and slid her fingernail under the cellophane tape. The box was plain and the message inside was typed on plain lined notebook paper.

"Babe?" J.D. prodded after giving her ample time to read the message.

Laurie blinked up at J.D. "I'm supposed to go to Palo Duro Canyon. To the Sad Monkey Train Station. But it's closed now."

"Sweetheart, I'm sure he prefers that no one witness the exchange."

Laurie felt as if she were swimming through mud. Her mind was so caught up in her emotions, she couldn't even decipher the simplest problem. J.D. had to explain everything to her like he would a rank amateur. Pitsie needed her clear-headed and in control. There was no way J.D. could come with her to the canyon.

It was billed as the "Little Grand Canyon," but there was nothing little about it. The canyon covered more than 16,000 acres and dropped to a depth of almost 800 feet. The deep walls, cut by years of erosion from the Prairie Dog Town Fork River, were especially spectacular at sunset, when the clear sun illuminated the varying colors of the soil.

Laurie and Pitsie had often driven the short distance out of town during the summer for the outdoor musical *Texas*, so Laurie was familiar with the basic layout of the park. The tiny road that wound its way through the canyon would lead her to the train station. The road was the main obstacle.

It was easily watched from any number of angles. In the flat open countyside surrounding the canyon, there was no way to hide a second car. If Nick had someone watching her, he could easily use binoculars to see in her car.

Even if J.D. tried to hide in the trunk, there would be no way for Laurie to get him out once they reached the station. He couldn't come with her and she wouldn't let him chance it.

"Laurie?"

She could tell by J.D.'s voice he had been talking to her for some time. "What time does it say to meet him?"

"Not until five. Guess he wants it to be almost dark."

"That gives us plenty of time to come up with a strategy," Henry stated positively. Laurie smiled at the grey-haired man and tried to stop her butterflies. This was her battle and as much as she hated it, she would have to fight it alone.

"Listen, you guys, if you don't mind I think I'll go back to the hotel and change clothes. Maybe try to rest." Laurie held up a hand to ward off their advice. "I know it's probably useless, but I just can't think right now. You two decide what our best course of action is and I'll agree."

J.D. looked torn. He obviously didn't want her to be alone, but he saw her reasoning. "Okay, sweetheart, if you think this is what you need to do. Call me if you need me and I'll see you about three or a quarter after to brief you." He kissed her lightly. "Could you ask Carrie to leave us alone?"

Laurie nodded and on impulse kissed the top of Henry's grey head. "I hope Margaret is as understanding."

"I don't think so. She took off when she saw you

sitting on Santa's lap. Something about it being disgusting."

"Sorry."

"Don't be." Henry waved her off and he and J.D. huddled over the desk.

Laurie noticed the gleam in J.D.'s eye but wisely decided not to comment on it. He had protested so vehemently against his former life, she knew he would deny the excitement pumping through him right now. She slipped out the door and headed for her hotel. J.D. sent Carrie out for lunch around one o'clock, but otherwise he and Henry allowed no distractions. They had over fifty years' experience between them and they were determined to keep Laurie's participation to a minimum.

"I think that's gonna be our best bet. Davidson will be expecting you to be with or follow Laurie, but he won't plan on me." Henry finally leaned back in the chair and picked at his teeth with the toothpick he had been chewing on for the past hour.

"Henry, I sure am glad I tackled you this morning. Since you're smaller than I am, you may be able to hunch down and not be seen in the car. I'll make a scene with my flat tire a few miles from the entrance. That should cause Davidson to lower his guard. He will think Laurie's back-up is delayed." J.D. never tore his gaze from the map they had acquired of the canyon.

"Hopefully by the time you're on your way again, I'll have had the time to slip out of the car and into all the underbrush," Henry said.

"Davidson should think he is in the clear. That's when I'll use the element of surprise. If we play this right, Laurie won't be in any real danger. Pitsie either."

Henry nodded. "That's the most important thing. I couldn't stand for either of those girls to be hurt. As much as I'd like to nail Davidson, the girls come first."

J.D. eased down in Laurie's chair and let his mind drift back over the past week. So much had happened this week. So many changes, good and bad.

"Somethin' bothering you, son?" Henry inquired.

"Yeah. I don't like the way Laurie just turned everything over to us. That's not like her. It's almost like she thinks we've lost before we've even begun to fight."

"You're right there. That one's a spitfire. Always has been according to her daddy. After that disaster with Ahadnad most people would've rolled over and died. Not our Laurie. By the time she got through reading them the riot act, even the White House felt the vibrations." Henry shook his head at the memory.

"You mean about her parents?"

"Yeah. When she found out her daddy had tried to talk to her immediate superiors and they wouldn't even see him, she hit the roof. You realize that if they had just talked to him, mentioned that Laurie was working on a classified assignment, her parents would be alive today. He thought Laurie was on leave. That's why they went over there. He really thought the government couldn't do anything."

J.D. clenched his fists. "So she quit."

"No. Not then." Henry glanced at the other man. He knew there were enough sparks flying between these two to start a three-alarm fire, but he hated to butt in. Heck, he'd gone this far, might as well go whole hog. "I figure she would've told you this already if things weren't so up in the air, but I guess it can't hurt for me to do it for her."

"Was it a dishonorable discharge?" J.D. held his breath.

"No, no, nothing like that. She did everything by the book, although she did write a few chapters of her own. No, the straw that broke the camel's back was the Corben case."

"I remember something about that."

"No wonder, it was in all the papers." Henry settled in for the tale. "Corben was a low-life sleaze that was helping ship classified documents out of the country. Laurie was to use her feminine wiles on him and infiltrate his set up. She's a beautiful woman so she had no trouble getting the old goat's attention. She acted like she was a girl with champagne taste on a beer drinker's pocketbook. Corben offered to help her make a little extra money."

"Bet I know how," J.D. growled.

"Oh, he wanted her to sleep with him all right, but he also wanted her help in getting the documents out of the country. Laurie knew the game goin' in. She told her boss she didn't mind letting him cop a feel but there was no way she was gonna sleep with him."

J.D. knew it was standard for some operatives to indulge in a little pillow talk but after what she had just gone through with Ahadnah, that was too much to expect.

"The bastards wouldn't listen. Without her knowledge they made it possible for Corben to be alone with her one time too many. The pig tried to rape her. I guess it was kinda like that date rape you hear about now."

J.D. clenched his fists and pounded them against his thigh. No wonder she had trouble being intimate. "Then she quit?"

Henry heard the harsh rasp of J.D.'s voice and decided it was a good thing he had been the one to inform J.D. of the situation. "No."

"What!" J.D. shot up out of the chair. "Why not?"

"Well, I guess maybe I misled you about that. She did quit but it wasn't over that. What finally got Laurie riled up was the Corben wife and kids. Her superiors had said that Corben was single and she had no reason to doubt them. They knew her well enough to know she wouldn't have flirted with him so convincingly if she knew he was married."

"But she was an agent. That goes with the territory."

"She knew that, too. She didn't really have a problem with the fact that he was married. What she did have a problem with was the fact that when the dirt hit the fan, Mrs. Corben shot her two sons and then killed herself."

"And Laurie blames herself."

"I suspect she does a little, but the part she couldn't handle was that Mrs. Corben found out on the late news. No one from any of the departments involved had even had the courtesy to inform her and help prepare her for what was to come. Laurie couldn't live with that. She even paid a visit to the President and bold as brass told him that there were some serious problems in the way the government operated. She made sure the Corbens were buried in the proper manner at the government's expense and then she turned over her retirement pay to the Corbens' girl. She had been at a party that night and survived to face all of it alone."

J.D. couldn't talk for the emotions choking him. He had known in the back of his head that something was wrong with Laurie's initial response to him. When he had accused her of being a tease, she hadn't slapped the dickens out of him like she should have, she had fallen apart. "She's one heck of a woman."

"You'll get no argument from me," Henry agreed.

"Think the two of us can pull this thing off?"

"We've got to, boy. I don't know who screwed up and decided Laurie Morrison was a terrorist, but I don't trust anyone."

"Then I guess we'll just have to do it."

FOURTEEN

Laurie maneuvered her car around an ice covered curve outside Amarillo. She had tried to go a little faster than she should and had slid all over the Interstate. She noticed the West Texas State University football stadium to her right and knew she only had a few miles to go before her turn-off to the canyon. Since the weather was so bad she figured the entrance would be closed, but that could work in her favor. If there wasn't anyone manning the booth, she could slip in unnoticed.

She took the exit and slipped her way down the unplowed roads to the park's entrance. The booth was empty and a white and orange saw horse blocked the way. It was simple to move the barricade and replace it.

The road was unmarred by car tracks and she wondered about Nick's mode of transportation. Of course, this wasn't the only way into the park.

She crept along the narrow twisting road past the scenic lookout and the amphitheater until she came to the turn off for the Sad Monkey Railroad Station. She and Pitsie had been here last summer and the place had been full of screaming boys and girls with tired parents.

She left the car in the parking lot and crunched across

the frozen ground. She noticed the train wasn't at the depot. She couldn't see anyone, but she could feel eyes on her.

The mesquite trees and bushes were merely black thorny branches covered with snow and ice. They resembled an evil forest from a picture book she had as a child.

Nick had instructed her to wait for the train to come into the depot. She was to place the money in the first car. Pitsie would be in the last car. The engineer would check the money and she could get Pitsie off the train. If she didn't follow the instructions, the engineer would blow the whistle and Nick's men would kill Pitsie.

Laurie's heart pounded as she heard the faint sound of the train on its journey. She strained her neck trying to catch a glimpse of it.

A snapping noise behind her sent her into a crouch and her hand dug into her coat pocket for the small pistol she had placed there. Her eyes scanned the bushes but to no avail. Even in the dead of winter the ground cover was too thick to see through and there were too many small buildings and rock formations for someone to hide behind. Laurie knew she was being watched, but from where?

The train was closer and she picked up the box of money she had dropped. She could finally see the train and she breathed a sigh of relief. It was almost over.

The person driving the train was completely covered in black so as to make any description impossible. Laurie couldn't even decipher the gender.

As the train slowed on its approach, Laurie leaned over the tracks to catch a glimpse of Pitsie. She refused to hand the box to the driver until she was sure Pitsie was safe.

The last car finally came into view. Empty! Did

Davidson think she was an idiot? The engineer held out his/her hand for the box but Laurie clutched it to her chest. Davidson could forget about his precious money until she had her sister.

"Where is she?" Laurie bellowed over the noise of the engine.

"Give me the box!" At least she knew it was a man now.

"Not until I have my sister." She backed away from the man and into a pair of strong arms. Thinking it was J.D., she spun around.

She found herself staring into a pair of mirrored sunglasses. The man holding her was dressed identically to the engineer. Crud, she had played right into Davidson's hands. She should have told J.D. the truth about the meeting time and he would be here right now. Fixing the mess she had gotten herself into.

The man reached into her coat pocket and pulled out her gun. He didn't say anything, but pitched the pistol into the bushes. He shook his head at her.

The strong arms pushed her along until she was forced to sit in the car behind the engineer. The man climbed into the seat behind her and she knew the hard point pressing into her back was a gun. Presumably bigger than the one she had carried.

"I'm sorry, Pitsie. I should have trusted J.D." Her words were a broken whisper heard only by the frozen wind.

J.D. adjusted himself into the saddle as his mount tried to descend a rather steep incline. He prayed the horse was as surefooted as its owner promised.

The old man was a friend of Henry's and hadn't even batted an eye when Henry told him he needed two horses to take into the canyon. J.D. figured the man would think they were crazy, but Henry explained people often took horses into the park. J.D. felt better knowing that this wasn't the first time his horse had trod over these snow-covered portions of ground.

Henry had taken another route to the depot to increase their chances of arriving at the depot unnoticed. The muscles in J.D.'s jaw twitched as he clenched and unclenched his teeth. His emotions were a battle ground at the moment. Anger and fear were battling for supremacy.

His anger at Laurie for pulling such a dunderheaded stunt battled with his fear for her safety. When Henry had knocked on the door and she hadn't answered he had used the connecting door again. She had been there, that was obvious by the dress flung across the end of the bed. He had noticed a note propped against the ashtray.

She was sorry about lying to him about the drop time but this was her fight and she couldn't let anyone risk their life.

J.D. realized she had been playing along with them in the office. He had roared out his anger to Henry, who sat calmly on the bed.

"Feel better?" Henry asked during a lull in his tantrum.

"Hell, no! She's gonna get killed. It's a good thing we stopped by early."

"I'm sure she felt enough people had died because of her."

J.D. thought about her parents and the Corbens and knew the old man was right.

Henry didn't give him any time to fume. He immediately began making new plans.

Henry had directed him to Mr. Johnson's ranch and within an hour they were traveling into the canyon on horseback. J.D. had to admit the old man knew his stuff. Because Henry had kept his mind together, they might have a chance at pulling this off yet.

His horse snorted and the sound echoed around them in the stillness. He reached down and stroked the coal black neck. He could see the depot at the bottom of the hill and he tugged on the reins. The horse stopped instantly and J.D. had to lock his knees against the straining sides of the animal to keep from flying over its head. It had been a long time since he had ridden anything without an engine.

The depot was nestled among the junipers but he could see Laurie pacing back and forth along the platform.

J.D. tethered the horse to a mesquite tree and slipped down the rest of the hill on foot. It was vital that he didn't alert anyone to his presence.

He kept a look-out for any sign of Henry, but so far he hadn't seen hide nor hair of the man. He hoped Henry had been able to navigate his way around the canyon.

He inched closer to the station. The ice-covered ground slowed his progress considerably and every footstep was a cacophony of snaps and crackles.

He slowly made his way to one of the small supply buildings situated a few feet from the platform. He leaned against the building trying to slow his breathing. He had held his breath for the past several minutes and his lungs burned for oxygen.

Just as he decided to sneak a peek at Laurie he heard a loud pop. He saw her spin into a crouch and her hand went to her pocket. She had brought a gun. Not that it would do her much good.

His ears picked up the sound of the train and he noticed that Laurie had become more agitated. The train began to pull into the station and J.D. caught a glimpse of the black-clothed engineer easing the train into the station. The man held out his hand for the box but Laurie shook her head. She leaned over the edge of the platform and stared at the rest of the train. The man became more insistent, but Laurie wouldn't budge. He could see her saying something to the man but she still held on to the money.

He noticed the rest of the train was empty. Evidently, Laurie had expected Pitsie to be a passenger.

J.D. noticed a black blur out of the corner of his eye. The engineer evidently had a twin brother. Laurie stepped back into the man's arms and J.D. stifled the urge to rush to her rescue.

Laurie was forced to board the little train and it began pulling away from the depot. J.D. hurriedly made his way to a batch of mesquite bushes lining the track. The long sharp thorns gouged into his arms and legs as he belly-crawled under them. He had to get on that train unnoticed.

The last car was almost to him as he reached the track. He sprang from his crouched position and slid into the small car. By keeping his knees curled under him and his head down he should go undetected. Unfortunately, he couldn't see what was happening.

His legs protested their cramped position and he tried flexing his muscles to keep the blood flowing. He could just envision leaping off the train and falling on his face when his knees buckled under him.

The train began slowing and J.D. slipped off the train. Sure enough, his legs buckled and he ended up with a mouth full of dirt. He swiped his hand across his mouth trying to clean it. He spat out what he could and swallowed the rest. Staying among the thorny underbrush, he inched along the track until he heard voices.

Laurie sat stock still in the car of the train trying to get her bearings. Neither man had uttered a word and she was grateful. She didn't want them to hear the terror in her voice. She had to stay in control.

The train slowed to a stop and Laurie noticed a large black pickup parked on one of the service roads. Pitsie sat in the back. Her mouth had been taped with gray duct tape and a bright red bandana was stretched tightly over her eyes. Laurie could tell by her awkward position that her hands were tied behind her back.

Pitsie's hair hung in limp strands and it looked greasy and uncombed. Laurie prayed that the lack of a shower had been the only hardship Pitsie had been forced to endure.

The man behind her jumped off the train and jerked her with him. His grip was unnecessarily cruel and she was glad she couldn't see his eyes. She knew they would portray a soul devoid of feeling or compassion.

"Bring the girl here." Laurie was amazed at the authority in her voice. Maybe her training would pay off after all. She certainly sounded in control.

"You're getting pushy again," the man growled and tore the package from her grip. He pitched the box to the engineer.

Laurie noticed the second man hesitated to rip open the package. "I followed your directions. It took me a while to ditch my friend, but he thinks we aren't meeting until five. That should give you plenty of time to get out of here."

"You're a very smart young woman. You say you picked up all this valuable information watching T.V.? The government could use someone like you."

Laurie could tell from the sarcasm in his voice that he was well aware of what she had been. Play time was over. "I'm sure you know precisely where I picked this up."

"Yes, Laurie, I am fully aware of your previous

career. Just as I am aware of who really pays Mr. Westat's bills."

"There isn't any need to worry about J.D. I was afraid he would come in here with guns blazing and end up dead. I didn't want that on my conscience."

"I don't suppose I could persuade you to come to work for my little organization? No? Oh, that is too bad. I'm sure we would work together much better than we have in the past." The man pushed her forward and her boots slipped on the ice covered ground, she tried in vain to regain her balance but ended face down at his feet. He chuckled at her discomfort. Great, just what she needed. Now he would think . . . What was that?

Just beneath the bushes edging the tracks Laurie caught a glimpse of movement. From her position on the ground she could barely recognize the outline of a man.

J.D.'s eyes shone like a beacon and Laurie quickly stood up. She had to be careful not to reveal his position. How had he gotten here so fast? She dared a casual glance in his direction, but she couldn't see him when she was standing.

"It's all here," the other man announced.

Laurie stiffened. That was Nick's voice. She spared a glance at the man holding her. She had been so sure Nick was in charge of this little kidnapping that it never occurred to her he had only been carrying out orders.

"Why the surprise, my dear. Could it be that you recognized my friend's voice?" The sunglasses reflected off her face as he stared at her. "Yes, I can see that is it. My goodness, you certainly are easy to read. You must have forgotten about how to hide you emotions."

If Laurie had harbored any hope of their captors letting them go, it died an early death. Now that they knew she had identified Nick, there was no way they would let her go.

"Can I say good-bye to my sister?"

The deep, maniacal chuckle sent shivers down her spine. "I don't see why not. I am a very fair man."

"Oh, I'm sure." Laurie's voice dripped with sarcasm, but she didn't see that it mattered. The man planned to murder her, so she could say whatever she pleased.

Pitsie was hauled out of the pickup and she stumbled to the ground. Laurie broke free and rushed to her. "Sweetie, it's Laurie. Honey, I'm so sorry."

Pitsie began to cry violently and Laurie gently pried the tape off her mouth. "I'm so scared. Is it all over?"

"Almost, honey." Laurie turned to glare at the man towering over them. "Can't we do without the cuffs? She can't hurt anyone."

The man motioned to Nick, who quickly removed the cuffs and untied Pitsie's blindfold. Laurie noticed he was very careful and knew he must still have some feeling for Pitsie. If she could use those feelings for their benefit, it would up the odds. "Thank you, Nick."

Nick swung around to face the man. "She knows who I am."

"So she does, but then the young one knew also."

"But I was gonna take her with me. She wanted to come." Laurie heard the pleading in Nick's voice and knew he was as scared of the man as she was. Nick began to rant and rave at the man. He began to list all of the plans he and Pitsie had made. The man never uttered a word, but after a few minutes of Nick's tantrum, he put a stop to it.

Laurie cringed and threw her arm around Pitsie as she saw the gun rise. Nick held his arms across his face as if to stop the powerful and deadly course of the bullet.

The man's aim was precise and Nick didn't have time to register the pain of a small bit of metal plunging its way into his heart. Laurie knew that while the tiny bullet might make a small hole as it entered the boy's chest, once inside it would explode, sending bits of metal spiraling through the delicate inner organs to abruptly end his life. There was only time for a slight spasm of agony as he fell at their feet.

Laurie pulled Pitsie tighter into her embrace when the girl became more hysterical. Her screams echoed off the high canyon walls and Laurie had to struggle to contain the quaking little body.

"It is too bad you recognized him. I guess you can add poor Nick to your death list."

"You would've killed him anyway." Of that she was certain.

"You're right, of course. Dear Nick had already served his purpose."

Laurie noticed J.D. inching his way toward them and pressed Pitsie's face into her shoulder to prevent her from seeing him.

"Can I take her to the truck? She's going into shock." Laurie tried to figure out a way to keep Pitsie out of the line of fire.

"Certainly, I don't want anything to happen to Pitsie. I have the most delightful plans for her." He motioned with his gun.

Laurie's head shot up and the breath left her body. "What do you mean?"

"I'm sure you realize what a good price a beautiful young white girl can bring?"

Laurie knew immediately he was talking about white slavery. She had been investigating the disappearance of several young girls when she had become involved with Jamal. She knew how much an innocent girl like Pitsie would bring on the open market. "You—"

"Yes, my dear, I am probably all of those colorful names your well-bred tongue won't allow you to say. But that is neither here nor there. I assume you realize that, while you are very beautiful, your market value is too low for me to bother with."

"You know what they say about assuming." Laurie heard J.D. growl the words as he flung himself at the man's gun. She cringed at the loud report of the pistol, but noticed the bullet had merely lodged itself into the already inert form of Nick Davidson.

Pitsie began screaming again and Laurie shoved her into the pickup. "Get out of here."

Pitsie shook her head from side to side. "I can't! I can't!"

Laurie wrenched open the door and stood on the running board to shake Pitsie. "I need you. You've got to go for help."

Laurie reached inside and started the engine. She placed Pitsie's hands on the steering wheel and hoped the girl would run on automatic for at least a few miles. It really wouldn't matter if she made it to Canyon or Amarillo as long as she was away from all this.

Pitsie slammed the pickup into reverse and spun her tires for a few minutes as she backed down the dirt packed road. The pickup rammed a trash can and several bushes as she turned around, but Laurie noticed she had it under control as she tore down the road.

Laurie turned back to the two men grappling on the ground. She looked around for the gun, but couldn't find it. Instead, she reached into the back of her pants and pulled out her switchblade. She had started carrying it after the break-in at the house. If J.D. would just break away from the man for a second, she could chance a throw.

J.D. tasted the grainy metallic mixture of blood and dirt as the man landed a blow that split his lip. His eye was already swelling shut and he was pretty sure his nose was broken. He had managed to knock off those blasted sunglasses, but he couldn't get a grasp on the mask. If this jerk was gonna kill him, he at least wanted to know who he was.

He had let the man's smugness get to him and had jumped him a little sooner than he should have. Now he was rolling around on the frozen ground fighting for his life instead of holding a gun on the man. His timing had been off and he just couldn't resist that smart aleck remark.

At least Pitsie and Laurie had gotten away. He heard the pickup barreling down the road. If he didn't have to worry about Laurie, maybe he could turn things in his favor. The man seemed to be tiring and J.D. hoped he could outlast him.

The two broke apart and J.D. took a few much needed breaths. He had lost his gun somewhere. He prepared to lower his head and charge when he felt rather than saw the knife slashing through the air.

It sailed past his ear, missing it by only inches, and sunk into the abdomen of the man standing in front of him. J.D. noticed the blade was completely buried and knew there would be very little that could save the man from an incredibly pain-filled death.

The man stood still and his cold grey eyes blinked in disbelief. His hand quivered above the knife, as if he couldn't bear to touch it. His leather-gloved hand clasped the handle and slowly removed it, along with what J.D. suspected were a few inches of intestine. Still the man stood.

J.D. had seen men like this before. The mind dulled the pain. J.D. watched the man gently swipe at the blood gushing from him. Slowly, the man began to chuckle. His laughter held none of the hysteria of a dying man.

J.D. noticed the man had finally begun to struggle to remain upright and his humanity propelled him to the man. J.D. took the knife and helped the man lie down.

He felt someone standing next to him and glanced up. "What are you doing here?"

"Saving your rear end." Laurie whispered the words. She had been terrified J.D. would move into the path of the knife. She had noticed the other man bend down to pick up J.D.'s lost .38, and felt she had to take the chance.

"I thought you and Pitsie were gone." J.D. cradled the dying man's head in his hand and lowered it to the ground. He noticed the glazed eyes and knew that the man had to be in a tremendous amount of pain, yet he didn't make a sound. He was well trained.

"I sent her for help." She pulled J.D.'s hand away from the now dead man and held it tightly. "Are you going to take off his mask?"

"Yeah." J.D. probed beneath the turtleneck of the black sweater and found the bottom of the ski mask. He needed both hands to pry off the mask but Laurie refused to relinquish his left hand. "I'll be da . . . dad-gummed."

"Clifton," J.D. said.

"Conway," Laurie said.

"Are you saying this was your boss?" J.D. asked.

Laurie nodded but couldn't seem to break eye contact with those dead grey eyes. "You mean he was also Clifton?"

"That son of a . . ." J.D. shot a look in Laurie's direction to see if she would comment on his near slip of the tongue, but her eyes were glued to Clifton's. J.D. reached out and lowered Clifton's eyelids, breaking the connection. He could feel Laurie shudder at the release. She had just killed a man and he wasn't sure how it was going to effect her. "You gonna be okay, babe?"

Laurie raised her eyes to his and felt a sudden warmth penetrate the horrible chill that racked her. "I hope so."

"Come here." J.D. pulled her into the circle of his embrace and hugged her. He didn't release her as they struggled to their feet. Laurie was glad. She wasn't sure her knees would hold her yet. "We better go find my sister."

Feeling her need for him, J.D. lowered his lips to hers in a kiss that was one of comfort and trust. Passion would come later.

"My goodness, isn't this a touching scene."

FIFTEEN

Laurie froze and turned to stare into a pair of very hostile black eyes. With a groan, she fell back against J.D. and he automatically stepped between her and the .357 pointed at her heart.

The hand holding the gun looked fragile and delicate, but one look into those crazed black eyes told him that the hand felt very comfortable wrapped around the deadly weapon. "You're the grandmother."

"No, I am much more than that." The whispered words were threatening.

"Margaret?" Laurie could scarcely believe the woman standing before them was the same Margaret Washburn she had coffee with this morning. But it was, unless Margaret had an evil twin sister, which at this point wouldn't have surprised her.

"You may address me as Most Serene Highness."

"Huh?" J.D. squeaked a very unmasculine squeak.

Margaret's eyes narrowed into tiny slits and her finger caressed the trigger. "You will show me the proper respect."

"I will?" J.D. said as irreverently as possible and Laurie jabbed him in the ribs with her elbow.

"Most Serene Highness, may I speak?" Laurie lowered her voice and head in what she hoped was a manner that would appease the woman's deluded mind.

"You may." Margaret preened at being given the attention.

"Could we ask for an explanation?"

"Oh, never fear, all will be made clear before I send you and your murdering lover to hell."

"But J.D. didn't kill anyone, I did!" Laurie realized Margaret must think J.D. had killed both men. "And Clifton or Conway or whoever he is killed Nick."

Margaret shrugged her shoulders. "It only saved me the trouble." Her upper lip curled in disgust. "It would be most unbecoming."

J.D. felt compelled to ask, "If it would be unbecoming to kill these two, what about us?"

"Ah, that is different. Your deaths will assure my place in the heavens. I must see you punished for your crimes."

Laurie was getting frantic. "I just told you I killed him."

"I do not speak of this American trash." Laurie thought for minute she was going to spit on the body. "I speak of my son."

"Who on earth is your son?" Laurie promptly forgot her lowered voice.

"The Most High Lord Master Jamal Mohammad Ahadnad." Her speech had taken on a different accent than the one Laurie had tried hard to decipher.

"I killed him five years ago. Why have you waited until now? My whereabouts haven't exactly been a state secret," J.D. asked.

"You are such a foolish man. Of course, I could have taken care of you years ago, but Allah had given me a mission."

Great, one of those loony tunes. "Just what was the message?"

Margaret chose to disregard J.D.'s manner. "After I was informed of my son's murder, I was inconsolable. I required special sleeping potions. When I was in my deep slumber, it was revealed what I must do."

"Kill me."

"J.D., would you hush?" Laurie was afraid he was going to get them killed before help got there. She had to keep Margaret talking.

Margaret took a deep breath and continued as if J.D. hadn't interrupted. "Before Jamal's incompetent guard was executed, he confessed that both J.D. Westat and the American woman had also been in my son's room before the other girl discovered his body."

"I killed Jamal. Laurie didn't have anything to do with it," J.D. insisted.

"She had everything to do with it," Margaret spat out. "She had weakened my son. He had become obsessed with her and she used him. I begged him not to bring her into my home, but she had already poisoned his mind." Margaret turned her eyes to Laurie. "I know you believe Jamal would have married you and given you my house, but I would have made sure that never happened."

"Lady, you're crazy. Laurie didn't want to be with Jamal, he kept her prisoner," J.D. blurted.

"Do not be absurd. Of course she wanted to be with Jamal. All women longed to be in his favor." Margaret spoke with such vehemence that a trail of spittle ran from the corner of her twisted lips. "My son was every woman's dream. This American led him from his true calling. She is as guilty as you. For the past five years I have eaten, slept, and breathed my mission. I have spent a great deal of money maneuvering you to this fate."

J.D. and Laurie stole a glance at each other but said nothing.

Margaret continued without really paying them any attention. "It was so simple to enlist the aid of Mr. Clifton. Anything for money, as you Americans say. Although you are not alone in that respect. I found most people have a very low price."

Margaret stopped abruptly as J.D. inched closer. "Stop."

He did.

"It was really amazingly easy to convince the world that my little group were terrorists. The western world is so weak in that respect. With Mr. Clifton's help I was able to keep an eye on Mr. Westat. When I discovered you were both from the same town it was a simple matter to dispatch her parents. But you wouldn't follow my plan." She turned hateful eyes on Laurie.

"Sorry."

"I needed you to come home, but you insisted on staying with your career. Of course, after Mr. Clifton arranged the death of that family, you came around." Margaret spared Laurie a smile. "I do hope you have enjoyed your guilt."

"You mean the Corbens were murdered." Laurie felt the ground begin to sway under her and J.D. held her tighter.

"Certainly. Something had to be done to push you over the edge. I needed you here."

Laurie didn't try to stem the tears that streamed down her cheeks and froze in the biting wind. The guilt she had carried for five years eased but did not disappear.

"Mr. Westat, I must commend you on your devotion to your grandmother." She giggled as J.D. stepped forward. "Don't you wish to hear the rest?"

"More of this divine plan?"

"Doesn't it strike you as the work of a superior that

my plan has worked so smoothly? Once you both returned home, it was simple. Mr. Clifton arranged to work with Laurie and Nick became close to the rest of her family. The only problem I had was determining the proper time." She looked very pleased with her story.

"So you're sayin' that this whole thing is just in the great scheme of things? Our karma, I suppose." J.D. was back to being irreverent.

"Nothing so unstable. You and the woman have been cleverly maneuvered for the last five years. I have known every move. This is not coincidence." Margaret suddenly decided she had said enough and raised the gun.

"Laurie!" J.D. shouted as she stepped in front of him. He grabbed her and pushed her behind him. He heard the gun blast and waited for the pain. Laurie jerked in his grasp and he knew the bullet had found her despite his efforts. *"No!"*

"I love you." Her eyes were glassy with pain and he could barely hear her words over the sound of a second shot. This time the pain was immediate and searing. His thigh felt like someone had set it on fire.

Laurie had gone limp in his arms and he could barely hold her as they fell to the ground. He heard a third report and longed for the bullet that would keep him from a life without Laurie. He must be close to death, for the bullet that must have hit him registered no pain. His vision faded from hazy to black and he held Laurie closer. "I love you."

SIXTEEN

Laurie twitched her nose at the odd smell. She tried to open her eyes, but someone had welded them shut. Her fingers were too heavy to move and someone had shoved cotton in her mouth.

Her eyelids finally parted enough to allow a blinding crack of light. She ached all over. Even thinking hurt. Her head was fuzzy and her thoughts wouldn't organize themselves into the proper order. She felt like a jigsaw puzzle, scattered into a million pieces. Why didn't J.D. fix it? "J.D.?"

J.D. raised his head off the back of the reclining chair he had been living in for the past two days. He stared at the woman lying on the bed. Had she said something? Careful of his bandaged left leg, he eased out of the chair and went to stand by her side.

Even as pale as she was, she looked better than when he had charged into the emergency room on Friday. The ambulance attendant had been forced to sedate him on the way to the hospital. He had regained consciousness and demanded to know where Laurie was. When the sedation wore off he came up yelling like a banshee again.

He had been so afraid that he had slept for days and that she had been buried. He had bellowed for answers and when a nurse asked if he were a relative he seriously thought about decking her. A small dark-haired doctor had come in and saved the nurse a broken nose.

"Where's Laurie? Have they buried her yet?" It seemed important that she not be buried until he could see her one more time.

"I sincerely hope not," the doctor had quipped and J.D. had threatened to give him the nurse's broken nose.

"Ms. Morrison is in surgery right now." The doctor avoided saying any more than that.

"Is she gonna be okay?" J.D. had known she had been hit, but he wasn't sure how bad.

"Mr. Westat, as advanced as medicine is, there are still no guarantees. I would like nothing better than to tell you that she will recover, but right now I'm afraid she only has a thirty percent chance of recovery at this time. She has lost a great deal of blood and there was some damage to her right rib cage and lung where the bullet entered."

"I want to see her." J.D. noticed the nurse open her mouth to protest, but the doctor headed her off.

"Mrs. Johnson, please bring me a wheelchair."

J.D. couldn't resist sticking his tongue out at the retreating figure of Nurse Johnson. He wished he could forego the chair, but while he was stubborn, he wasn't stupid.

The doctor confirmed that Laurie was in recovery. After dressing J.D. in sterile clothing, they allowed him a few minutes with her. When Laurie had been placed in the ICU, Henry had pulled a few strings so that J.D. could stay with her. He hadn't left her side since. He hated the machines surrounding her. He couldn't stand the constant beep-beep of the heart monitor, but he found himself waking at all hours of the night listening for its reassuring irritation.

Now he was afraid he had conjured up Laurie's voice in his mind. He had begged her to give him some sign she was coming back to him. The doctor assured him her chances were improving, but there was still a chance of infection.

Laurie's eyelashes fluttered slightly but didn't open. "Come on, babe, it's time to wake up."

Laurie heard J.D. talking to her, but it was a really bad connection. She couldn't make out the words and for some reason her hand hurt. She tried moving her fingers from the vise-like hold.

J.D. felt the small twitch of her fingers and loosened his grip. Her lips curved into a relieved smile. "Thanks."

"Laurie!" J.D. shouted. "Laurie!"

The connection had cleared and she could hear him much better now. If only she could get the cotton out of her mouth, she could talk to him. Find out what was going on. She tried once more, but she was just so tired.

J.D. felt her relax and he tensed, waiting for the beep-beep to cease. Mercifully it kept its irritating rhythm. He reached over and pushed the nurse call. He hoped the nurses wouldn't think he had made the entire thing up.

They didn't and within minutes the doctor was shining his pen light in Laurie's eyes. J.D. took the time to step into the hall and talk to Pitsie.

"Hey, kiddo, how ya holdin' up?" He hobbled to the waiting room with a crutch tucked under his arm.

"Is she better?" Pitsie asked.

"Yeah, I think she's coming out of it. At least I got a little response." He reached over and ruffled her hair. She had changed dramatically in the last three days. Gone was the smart mouth and invincible attitude. She had come very close to dying and she knew it. J.D. figured she had been forced to grow up sooner than she should have and he was determined to help her through the days ahead.

The doctor told them they could see Laurie and Pitsie started crying again. J.D. didn't think he had ever seen anyone cry like she could.

Laurie was sitting up slightly and she smiled when she saw them. "I understand you've been making a nuisance of yourself."

J.D. grinned and raised her hand to his lips. "Not me."

Laurie turned her attention to Pitsie and after several minutes of hugs and kisses, the young girl left them alone.

"I hope you're more informative than the good doctor," Laurie said.

"What do you want to know?" He eased one of the hard-backed chairs close to the bed.

"Why aren't we dead?"

"Shi . . . shoot, you come right out with it, don't you?" He dropped her hand and rubbed the back of his neck. How much did she remember? What should he tell her? What should he leave out? In the end he told her everything.

"So Henry shot Margaret before she could finish us off?" she stated matter-of-factly.

"Do you have to keep talking like that?" J.D. shifted in his chair.

"Like what? I'm only stating the facts." Laurie took pity on the big, macho man. "Okay, Henry terminated Margaret with extreme prejudice before she completed her divine mission."

"Something like that. He got lost in the canyon or she probably wouldn't have gotten the first two shots off." He grinned as he thought of Henry berating himself. He had apologized to J.D. so often J.D. had taken to avoiding the man.

"Then it's over." Laurie leaned back into her pillow and closed her eyes. The doctor had said she would have to stay in the hospital for several days and then it would be weeks, maybe months, before she was back to normal. She had felt like telling him she would never be normal again. Her life had changed too dramatically. There was no way she could go back to being the person she had been before. "When do you leave?"

The question threw J.D. "I wasn't planning on going anywhere."

"What about TAT? Won't they put you on another assignment?" She held her breath. He wasn't planning on leaving. Did he want to stay? Did he want to stay with her?

"I put in for full retirement. I thought I'd stay here, if that's okay with you." His eyes searched her face for some sign.

"It's okay with me but I don't think Nurse Johnson will like it." He wanted to be with her. She could joke. She could relax. She could live.

EPILOGUE

The light from the television flickered over J.D.'s face as he made his way up to Laurie's spine. She shivered as the quilt slipped down past her hips.

"You cold?" His breath fanned her shoulder blade and he readjusted the quilt over them.

"Shh. This is it." Laurie reached for the remote control and turned up the volume.

The newscaster was relating the story of an anonymous donation to the children's home. A small, gaily wrapped package had been delivered to the home for Christmas Eve. The package contained several thousand dollars. The home had been facing a possible closing and the money would enable the home to continue to provide the much needed care it was responsible for. The reporter interviewed one little boy who claimed that he had asked Santa to help. The reporter stated that it had renewed his faith in the jolly old man.

"Mine, too," Laurie said, switching off the set. She rolled over and watched the play of the blinking Christmas tree lights on J.D.'s skin. He was magnificent.

"And did you get what you asked for?" he asked from the hollow of her neck.

Laurie thought over the last three weeks. Bubba had been granted an emergency leave and he wouldn't have to leave until after New Year's. Pitsie had become a veritable paragon of virtue. She had been promoted to mall manager and Henry had begun escorting Gloria around town.

All the government agencies had had all their questions answered and J.D. was officially one of the private sector. He had used his retirement fund to buy a security agency and he was still responsible for the security at the mall.

She glanced around at her newly redecorated living room and thought of the gorgeous bedspread adorning her new bed.

Most of all she thought of the man who had become such an intrinsic part of all their lives. He had destroyed her demons and shown her all that was glorious and good about life and love.

She noticed the twinkling lights reflect off the diamond on her left hand. "More than I ever thought about asking for. More than I ever dreamed existed."

SHARE THE FUN ...
SHARE YOUR NEW-FOUND TREASURE!!

You don't want to let your new book out of your sight? That's okay. Your friends can get their own. Order below.

No. 37 ROSES by Caitlin Randall
K.C. and Brett join forces to find who is stealing Brett's designs. But who will help them both when they find their hearts are stolen too?

No. 38 HEARTS COLLIDE by Ann Patrick
Matthew knew he was in trouble when he crashed into Paula's car but he never dreamed it would be this much trouble!

No. 39 QUINN'S INHERITANCE by Judi Lind
Quinn and Gabe find they are to share in a fortune. What they find is that they share much, much more—and it's priceless!

No. 40 CATCH A RISING STAR by Laura Phillips
Fame and fortune are great but Justin finds they are not enough. Beth, a red-haired, green-eyed bundle of independence, is his greatest treasure.

No. 41 SPIDER'S WEB by Allie Jordan
Silvia's quiet life explodes when Fletcher shows up on her doorstep.

No. 42 TRUE COLORS by Dixie DuBois
Julian helps Nikki find herself again but will she have room for him?

No. 43 DUET by Patricia Collinge
Two parts of a puzzle, Adam & Marina glue their lives together with love.

No. 44 DEADLY COINCIDENCE by Denise Richards
J.D.'s instincts tell him he's not wrong; Laurie's heart says trust him.

Kismet Romances
Dept 591, P. O. Box 41820, Philadelphia, PA 19101-9828

Please send the books I've indicated below. Check or money order only—no cash, stamps or C.O.D.'s (PA residents, add 6% sales tax). I am enclosing $2.75 plus 75¢ handling fee for each book ordered.

Total Amount Enclosed: $_____.

____No. 37   ____No. 39   ____No. 41   ____No. 43
____No. 38   ____No. 40   ____No. 42   ____No. 44

Please Print:
Name_____
Address_____ Apt. No._____
City/State_____ Zip_____

Allow four to six weeks for delivery. Quantities limited.